Not In Her Majesty's Service

Guenther Focke

authorHOUSE®

AuthorHouse™ UK Ltd.
500 Avebury Boulevard
Central Milton Keynes, MK9 2BE
www.authorhouse.co.uk
Phone: 08001974150

All rights of distribution, including by printed media, film, radio and television, photo mechanical report, sound storage media of any kind, a part reproduction or input and recovery in data-processing systems of all kind are reserved.

© 2008 Guenther Focke. All Rights Reserved.

No part of this book may be reproduced, stored in a retrieval system, or transmitted by any means without the written permission of the author.

First published by AuthorHouse 9/8/2008

ISBN: 978-1-4389-1660-6 (sc)

Printed in the United States of America
Bloomington, Indiana

This book is printed on acid-free paper.

This book was originally published in German with great success by MatrixMedia (Göttingen). The author wishes to thank MatrixMedia for relinquishing all rights & responsibilities in connection with the publication of the English-language version.

Internet: www.guenther.co.uk

Author's Preface

On this day now that I begin to write this down, I start to realize how interwoven life can be and how things can happen (and sometimes, I have to confess, some pretty mad things) that lead you away from basic questions, then lead you back to them. Again and again have I been reminded by coincidence of my own case ... maybe while searching for a lost young girl in the forests and moors near Lands End in south-western England or in the course of other investigations which often enough dealt with the search for the real identity of a person, like once in Brazil. In a way, I have learnt through my investigative work to discover and evaluate my own case over and over again. In many of those investigations and inquiries one basic question appeared to be desperately waiting to be answered, the question of who we are and what we do. Furthermore, why we do things one way and not another ... whoever undertakes investigations into one's own origins is looking for a place, a story and a conversation with the past, accompanied - and in the end - determined by one's self.

My investigations have indeed guided me to my real origin. Evidence and witnesses refer to Prince Philip, husband of Her Majesty Queen Elizabeth II. Since the mid 90's they have been leading me directly to Buckingham Palace.

I have appeared before the public with my findings and documentation. No other way was possible, as Buckingham Palace's policy was to continuously refuse to acknowledge my findings and to forbid their publication. I received anonymous threats to my life and I do not know who was responsible for this. Then again, I always felt that I had been treated with courtesy and respect during my communications with Buckingham Palace.

For over a decade I thought about publishing my story, but the question was how I should put pen to paper and write it all down. After long conversations with publishers, friends and insiders it became clear to me that I had to publish my story in a way that respected the historical and socio-political rules and regulations in connection with the British Crown.

My desire to search for the truth and to honestly proclaim it should not be misunderstood as a provocation of the British Crown, instead it should be taken as something that can be proven and, in the end, be viewed as the noble right I believe it is.

All names used within this book were changed except the one of my investigation teacher and mentor Wolfgang Xanke, as well as any named authors.

As I wanted to make it clear that this is not fiction, but the true story of my life, I have attached copies of my exchange of letters with Buckingham Palace, also records of the movements of the ship HMS Whelp with an extract of the actual manning list of the Royal Navy at the end of the book, in addition to a family tree and a list of referenced literature.

February 2006

Günther Focke

Dawn arose when I decided to go to the lake to fulfill my desire of feeling the air touch my cheeks and cooling my brow. Often at this time silence spread through the night, when Sir Arthur White and I hushed along the embankment. My glance spread over the lake, little drifts of ice floating northward. You can see ducks peacefully resting on them. In the West the light still has a dark-blue taint, with thin rose-colored stripes of the rising sun forming the horizon in the far southeast. The crowns of poplars are all frozen. You hear little branches and twigs crackling in the wind. Cold air is cutting and biting my ears. It was cold at Loch Linnhe in Scotland.

It was one of Arthur White's characteristics to hold his Round Table in ruins, castles and sometimes even in improvised Bedouin tents. He was able to afford a whole castle for a weekend. Maybe it belongs to him. After several meetings nobody asked if only five rooms or even the whole castle was rented. Nobody really wanted to know. We met every three months in a small group of four or five. The host himself, Sir Arthur White, a lawyer back then, then the Spanish investment broker Miguel Xavier, the theologian Reverend Mill, and then of all people me, Günther Focke. It was most likely thanks to the Reverend Mill that I was sometimes invited to these meetings. He is still a good old friend of mine.

It was he who consoled me in times of deepest desperation by saying that everything will work out fine, even if the quest for my identity and origin would make my memories turn my world upside down up to the point where God Almighty would one day relieve me from my pain.

Miguel was of the same opinion, » Focke! You old fool! You are like an angel from medieval times, forgotten by God to be brought back home. What are you still doing here? « He often used to say. Then he would always hand me a Cuban cigar with a smile to make up for his outspoken comment.

He was a rogue of the highest degree, but at times he was very serious. Arthur and he formed a coalition against me the night before. I decided to completely reveal myself to them and to report that some time after my meeting in London I received a package that had a substance in it … which leaked when I opened the package … which almost killed me.

Had I turned into such an enemy of the British Empire, or to put it better, an enemy of a selected circle of people? Me, the little Günther Focke, who grew up in a small town on the North Sea coast of Germany one year after the Allies had defeated the Third Reich and being called 'Tommie' by the local kids and adults alike.

This curse was to be the trap door of my life, because I was born as a son of an Englishman in autumn 1945. They told me he was a British Navy officer. His identity: Prince Philip, married to Queen Elizabeth II since 1947.

»For God's Sake, Günther, an attack on your life right after your encounter with one of the private secretaries of Buckingham Palace. Are you aware of what you are saying; are you aware of what consequences this could have? «, my beloved Mill replied coming toward me and grabbing my hand. Arthur remained silent sucking on his cigar and creating a mountain of smoke around himself. I looked around. There was silence. The only sound was the back-and-forth movement of the pendulum in the large grandfather clock.

After a while Xavier started to tap his boot heels in rhythm, then he leaned over in his chair, folded his hands and said, »Senor Günther, don't you want to stop this game, this hunting game to find out about your background? Believe me; the British Crown will never admit that you are the pre-marital son of Prince Philip! «

»He thinks he will find himself if he finds his origins. For him it is all about the truth of reality«, Mill said.

»Truth of reality? «, Miguel added in a theatrical manner, » it is all the construction of two accomplices, Zeitgeist and power! And you know what I mean when I refer to power! «

Arthur cleared his throat and put his cigar down on the marble ash-tray. » Dear friends, it was a wise man, I think his name was Walter Bageshot, who in 1867 wrote about the role of the monarchy in "The English Constitution", saying: "We can not let daylight fall onto the monarchy!" And this is how it will stay forever.

It is good that especially these days the highest ranks amongst the monarchy learn to be masters of their own roles and live outside the boundaries of what we conceive to be the norm. «

»But on the other hand the monarchy is also completely imbedded and present in our every day media democracy. Not one day passes without some scandal or another being published in the gutter press. This kind of entertainment is also a type of opium for the people. «, the Spaniard replied.

»If the highest heads and governments, and this of course includes everyone including the Pope in Rome, gave up their roles, Sodom und Gomorrah would reign. The people need a real picture of the almighty. Everybody is set out to be king. In order for this not to just be an idea, there has to be visible reality of this idea«, was the Reverend Mill's reply.

»Oh, Mill, you old early romantic«, Miguel said, » you quote Friedrich von Hardenberg, known as Novelist. That was so long ago. Did you forget about what happened over the last 200 years? None of those responsible follow ideals any more, they only think of how they can conserve the continuity of their crazy species - if this is possible at all. Who is still interested in ideals? You have those who fight through dirt and dust in order to survive, those who fight to survive in factories producing consumer goods to the thousands and others who are only out to find a cheap face-lift from the Internet. «

» So is it all about continuity? «, Arthur added, » what do you think would happen if the British Crown abdicated and the Vatican turned into a Museum? «
» Financial chaos! «, was Miguel's reply, » Tourism, the hotel industry, the airline industry, dealing in art and a lot more would collapse. «

» What would Rome be without the Vatican? « Mill asked, »what about all the art treasures in the Palazzo Vecchio in Florence, what about Michelangelo or Rafael without the Pope? The same would occur for London and its traditional allies. Without the British Crown all around us would, all of a sudden, belong to the past and all of us would only be museum guards of our nations«.

» And there is more, my friends, there is more «, Arthur warned lifting his forefinger, » a part of our own perception would get lost. Important personalities like the British Crown and the Pope in Rome represent living metaphors of our culture and history of our civilization. They silently bear our thoughts and feelings by speaking and acting to the world expressing our own perception of things. You should also bear in mind that the Queen is not only Queen of England, but also head of the Anglican Church and the Commonwealth. Top secret documents go via her office. Her Majesty furthermore connects Canada, Great Britain and Australia. The importance of the Pope in Rome is indisputable, especially during these times of religious conflicts between Christians, Jews and Muslims. «

»In the sixties we would have never thought about something comparable to a renaissance of religious belief. Back then it was 'in' to be a Marxist or anarchist and to deny any honorable moments of tradition and self-conception «, Mill explained.

»Yes«, added Arthur, »you eventually start to think about your own values when nothing remains from the illusions and experiments of modern times«.

»Arthur«, I said, »You all pretend as if my small existence contradicts the one you have so nicely documented. But that is not the case. I am not that kind of rebel who expresses discontent about the different systems. Do you really mean that I am not allowed to investigate the fact of His Royal Highness, Prince Philip, being my father? «

» Günther, we know that you became a private detective just because you wanted to be able to explore your background. I do not have a problem with this, but we are not in favor of you going public with it! «, my friend Mill explained.

By that time it was already too late for his advice. I had already drawn attention to myself as a guest on various German TV shows, one with Thomas Gottschalk and the other with Sandra Maischberger, furthermore, the German newspaper BILD and other media organizations had already run stories on me.

» Mill! «, I said, » if I had not already made it public we wouldn't have sat here and discussed all these facts about me. You cannot simply call up Buckingham Palace as a 'nobody' and say: Hello! I am the illegitimate son of Prince Philip! And I would like to prove my case! This would only be possible if you made it public before! «

» So then «, Arthur replied, » the public and the reaction of Buckingham Palace would be part of the detective work in order to find out if your allegations are really true? «

» Sorry, Arthur, but I quickly have to intervene«, Miguel interrupted, »You still have not told us about how you, Senor Focke, came up with this insane idea that Prince Philip may have fathered you? If so, then why? Did he not have better things to do? And where should these allegations have taken place? «

» This was in Wremen, a small town between Bremerhaven and Cuxhaven, in October/November 1945. After the war the British and the American Army were stationed there! «, I started to report. » The reason they chose Wremen was because it was geographically the best place to have military control over the mouth of the Weser. Wremen was a strategic base and a lot of supply and other traffic passed through this town. «

» Are there any witnesses who confirm Prince Philip being your father? «, Miguel asked.

» Yes, my aunt Auguste, as well as Heiner Kleinert, who in his own words said: 'why does Prince Philip not admit that he has been here before, we all know about it! « My mother, Marie-Karoline Focke worked in a pub called Schwanewedel back then. Civilians and military people got together there. And the British Naval Officer Prince Philip - as it is well known - was very close to her. Apart from this fact, there are other indications.

When I was a child, I was given a photo, but they later destroyed it with the remark that he would never return anyway, because he was a nobleman married to a very powerful lady in England. This was in 1947. And the information came from the newspaper Nordsee Zeitung. As a matter of fact I was able to find an article of the Nordsee Zeitung dating back to this time where no other aristocratic or noble people were mentioned for getting married in 1947 ... except for the Royal couple. «

» Günther «, now Arthur remarked, » you just said that your making it public is part of your detective work and that you afterwards got in contact with Buckingham Palace. What exactly did happen? And how did you leave it? «

» Oh, for that I have to go back into more detail «, I started, » yes, there are phone calls, exchanges of letters and a meeting with the private secretary of Prince Philip.

It was my first real contact. On April 19th 1995 at 11.30am, Brigadier Sir David Lang-Smith and I had an appointment at the Army & Navy Club, Pall Mall in London. Of course, I was there an hour early so that I could get a proper feel for this club.

As was to be presumed, the atmosphere was very silent, sterling and British. The club was decorated in a slight Victorian style. When you entered the club you stood directly in front of the reception. On the right was the coffee room. I sat down in a leather armchair, lit a cigarette and observed the people, the waiters, the way they moved around, their mimics and their gestures.

It was a mixed bunch of people, partly civilians and partly people in uniform. The place was obviously very male-dominated. They were sitting or standing, one gentleman was wearing a kilt. All of them were smoking cigars and exchanging pleasantries as a matter of course. Every once in a while one gentleman would show a surprised look to a comment made here and there. The general atmosphere was however unconcerned. You could tell by the body language and facial expressions that they were part of a kind of trained communication ritual, which was set to a certain standard from which no one deviated. It was not the way they were dressed - it was more the behavioral patterns that made these club members belong to this particular inner circle.

I looked down on myself to check whether my dress attire was appropriate enough so as not to be recognized at first sight as Günther Focke. I realized the hidden looks, of course, which hit me from the corner of the officer's eyes. Everybody was completely lost in their talks. The only one sitting on his own was me, not reading the newspaper and obviously waiting for somebody.

I was just about to light another cigarette when right at this moment Brigadier Sir David Lang-Smith finally came up to me. He acted as if he were somewhat important, trying to distract from the awkward and unreal atmosphere this situation created.

As soon as he sat down a waiter came rushing by. They knew each other, he then ordered. I still had some coffee and biscuits.

» Mr. Focke «, he started, » all you say is really interesting, but I am afraid – let's put it this way: the magnetism of the Palace will get you into trouble.

We would like to help you on the search of your real father; however we are limited in our possibilities. «

» I understand «, I replied, not comprehending a word he said. What did he mean by referring to 'the magnetism' of the Palace?

» Sir David «, I then explained, » I have been searching for the identity of my father for decades now and believe me, my findings - which also include confidential testimonies - give me enough evidence to argue that I am the son of H.R.H Prince Philip. «

»Maybe, Mister Focke, in your youth you and H.R.H Prince Philip may have looked alike, but have you got proof that would stand up in a court of law? «

» The trail leads to Buckingham Palace «, I said.

» If you do not have any proof you should be aware that if you do not have anything to base your allegations on, the Palace will not tolerate this under any circumstances. «

His voice became sterner. Was it his intention to provoke me? Or, to make me show all my cards telling him about the witnesses who are able to prove my allegations are not unfounded. What if I can in fact verify that Prince Philip was not in Melbourne at this time, contradicting his claims of 1995?

I did at least plan to offer him evidence that proves the statement of Prince Philip to be wrong:

» In an interview Prince Philip has stated that he was in Melbourne in September. There is a book that says he left England in September 1945. «

» Really? «, he now seemed to be a little surprised, » and who wrote this book? «

» His name is Tim Heald! «, I answered.

» Don't you think that you sound provocative, Mister Focke? «

I don't want to provoke anybody, please understand Brigadier, I don't want to step on anyone's toes! But what would you do in my place, when you are surrounded by facts like this almost every day. «

He smiled and leaned back. » Certainty, Mr. Focke, is not only a question of feelings or mood, but also a question of shape, the form of a thought. I have to concede, though, that your intention is friendly. I will investigate this case personally «.

He quickly finished his tea and looked me straight in the eye. Then he stood up said good bye and left. I just sat there totally astonished.

And in fact shortly after this meeting I received a letter from him stating that he did some research and is able to say full of certainty that Prince Philip could not have been in Europe during the period in question. Of course, I was not expecting anything else. The Palace again proved to be pleasant and conscientious, I thought. «
» Magnetism! «, Arthur said, » Yes, indeed, the Palace is surrounded by strong magnetism!

No wonder! But, Günther, the question is, where was Prince Philip really at the time you were conceived? «

» The question of all questions «, Reverend Mill repeated.

» Of course I have investigated what was written about him. Interestingly enough there are several documents - including books - about him being in England and Europe during this time. I was able to find another book by someone called Cramer. This book is fairly old, published shortly after the end of WWII. It says, that Prince Philip telegraphed Princess Elizabeth in early 1945 that he would soon return to England.

But all of these were published before I went public. Subsequently to 1995/96, all publications indicate that he was on the fleet destroyer HMS Whelp stationed in the Pacific well into 1946. For example, a different book with the title Philip and Elizabeth, portrait of a marriage, by Gyles Brandreth, - a royal court author and writer, states that Philip said he came back to England one year after the capitulation of Japan. The book was published for the first time in 2004. In here the interview matches what Prince Philip first said in a television interview in 1995, which is that he was in Melbourne on the HMS Whelp and the aircraft carrier HMS Illustrious for maintenance work during the time in question. «
» A very interesting discrepancy «, Miguel added.

» Correct «, I replied, » out of all the existing documents there is no proof up to now. And according to the testimony of Frank William Blair this claim is completely wrong. So, one discrepancy leads to another one. «

» Who is this Blair? «, Arthur asked.

»I was able to find him via log books and ship movements. I was even able to meet him and to talk to him personally in England. Back then, he was in Melbourne on the wharf and he told me that the HMS Whelp was not in harbor there during this time. The wharf was only small and easy to overview. He told me that Japanese prisoners of war did not start building this wharf until 1945. «, I explained.

Miguel argued: » I really cannot believe that you, dear Focke, could be the reason for an entire change of the historical background of Prince Philip. Buckingham Palace has come up against many accusations. You, however, are only small in comparison. What is the reason for this discrepancy? Maybe because you exist? A little misconduct, or even better why don't we call it an adventure of His Royal Highness before marrying Elizabeth II.? Are there any other reasons given that indicate why His Royal Highness definitely needed to be in Melbourne during this period? What if your existence is not the real reason that historically placed Prince Philip in Melbourne at this time; maybe this was to avoid the public knowing about his real whereabouts for a totally different reason?

You, dear Günther Focke, would only represent the publicity side any such revelation would bring, which could be avoided. What exactly do they want to keep a secret? Only you … or maybe something else? «

» Our Miguel has always been a good one to put a theory to this kind of situation, this is all part of being a stock broker«, Arthur said, making fun of him.

» Ah, dear Sir Arthur, the one who is the first to laugh and laughs the loudest is the one who has something to hide! «, Miguel answered back.

» I still have to tell you something! «, I started again, » Not long ago I tried to get back a book from a well known author in the United States. Her name is Kitty Kelly. I had lent it to her for a long time, with some film material, which was however all copied. This biography about Prince Philip is written by Tim Heald. In this book it also says that Prince Philip left England in 1945. When I could not get hold of Kitty, I decided to buy the book again. But when I tried to find this passage that I am referring to, I could not find it, regardless how often I read through the book. It looked like they had deleted this part of the book. I called the publisher and asked why this had happened.

They told me, that I had bought a new edition. Obviously there had been minor changes made to the book. So I tried to somehow obtain the original version again, going from one book shop to another. The book was completely sold out. It had simply disappeared, as simple as that, just like that...gone! «

» Günther «, Mill started to say, »since when has the edition disappeared? «

» To tell you the truth shortly after I met with Brigadier Sir David Lang-Smith and told him about this book and this special passage about Prince Philip having left England in September 1945 «.

» What a coincidence «, countered Arthur, » but what can this prove? Do you want to say, that all the books relating to Prince Philip and his stay near Germany during the time when you were conceived have all disappeared? «

» But listen Arthur, it is interesting to see « , Miguel intervenes, » that the facts were obviously manipulated in favor of Buckingham Palace; I know it is nothing more than speculation, but there is also some logic to it all. «
» I was able, by the way, to get an old edition in a tiny obscure antique shop «, I continued, » here now, in this edition, it still says what I had previously said to be the case. That he was not in Melbourne. In September he left England. «

» Günther «, Reverend Mill turned to me now and looked at me very seriously, » at the beginning you said that someone tried to eliminate you. Do you feel like speaking about this matter? «

» Dear friends, this is not an interrogation and not a hearing «, Arthur interdicted, » there are some things I don't even want to know about! «

Mill, Miguel and I stared at Arthur who was lighting another cigar.

Of course he knew that we were looking at him with unanswered questions still in the air, but this did not distract him from lighting his cigar in his usual and nearly ceremonial way.

Arthur took his thick horn-rimmed glasses off, cleaned them with a red and white chequered silk cloth and said, » Günther, I know that you think about perhaps publishing this conversation of the four of us. It will be difficult to reproduce every detail we have talked about. Do you know why? This is because you do not have the scientific and historical background. It does not really matter, but keep this in mind, the general public will not believe you if you plan to reveal this situation with you and the connection with the Palace. It will only result in humiliation for you. And seriously, Günther, do you really think the Palace would be so stupid and try to get rid of you? «

» Maybe it is not the Palace, but somebody else? « Miguel whispered to himself.

» Eager loyalists sometimes work without authorization of their crown, I know about examples in the history of the church «, Mill mentioned.

» Are you talking about people in the background, who follow situations like this? «, Arthur asked.

» Well «, I interrupted, » I nearly believed that somebody indirectly communicated with me in these publications about Prince Philip after 1994. I did in fact read about some obscure men behind Buckingham Palace, who manage and sort out certain affairs without anyone knowing anything about it. «

Arthur started to laugh: » That is lunacy! Günther! You are totally paranoid! «

» Please, give us an example! « Mill stated.

» Well, – what was his name again? Gyles Brandreth, for example: In the very first sentence of the introduction it says the author was introduced to the Queen by Prince Philip himself. He is a royal court author. Why not then? Why is there all this over-the-top journalistic investigation work covering rumors of Prince Philip and his possible infidelities and premarital affairs? Brandreth mentions an Australian woman by the name of

Robin Dalton. In contradiction to what Prince Philip's friend and confidant Michael Parker said, she claimed, that it was commonplace to have a certain promiscuity between unmarried people in the South Pacific in 1945 «, I reported.

» Yes, this is all about the construction of history and the past! A lovely girlfriend of mine always gives me a lecture about being subjective in relation to past memories « Miguel added with a laugh.

» The question is not about being selective of someone's memory, but about whether this passage is in the book or not, Senor «, Reverend Mill corrected him.

» Yes I know, Mill «, replied Miguel.

I tried again to find a conclusion to my thoughts: » Anyway, there are several parts in this book that deal with the so called premarital affairs of Prince Philip, more so that in the end they can say: no, no, nothing like that happened. I read different passages over and over again in order to find hidden implications, perhaps only indicated by a question mark. Whilst reading it something completely different caught my eye, namely how much the rhythm of language is compromised whenever the subject matter is delicate?

For example during a vacation of Prince Philip and his friend Michael Parker in Australia and North Africa. In between I had the impression, that the author papered over any loopholes and tried to divert attention from any paradox or strange things in his storyline by adding some witty and amusing comments that were out of place - as if you were reading hundreds of pages of a historical and factual text and then suddenly out of nowhere someone comes up with: Hot dogs! «

» The German origin is still deep in you. You can't understand that. We British sometimes express ourselves in strange ways. « The Reverend replied.

»Senor Focke, the way I know you; you are sure to have been very meticulous when putting together the bibliographical documentation about your assumed father and evaluating this material. If we were to put these - indeed, thrilling - speculations aside and again focused on solid facts, what would your research findings come to? We can only act on the assumption that the Palace's information policy about Prince Philip's whereabouts in 1945 changed after your story entered the public domain in 1994. What can you tell us about these facts here? «

» Well, these are all fragments which do not really draw a precise picture of Prince Philip's whereabouts. «, I explained, » there are text passages indicating that during the war Prince Philip met Princess Elizabeth several times in Windsor. So he must have had connections that enabled him to come back to northern Europe even during the war.

In the same book - published in 2004 - you can find the passage where it is described that until the year 1946, when he came to Balmoral one year after the end of the war, he never seriously thought about getting married. As already mentioned, Brandreth writes about this. «

» It is no discrepancy to come back to Balmoral one year after the war ended after patrolling the German North Sea coast for a while «, Miguel said, » I would have done the same if I had been in his shoes and it had become clear to me that I was to marry the heir to the throne. «

» Oh well «, I countered, » it is not that easy. In Hugo Vicker's book about Alice of Battenberg, Princess of Greece, published in 2000, it says explicitly, that at the end of the war Prince Philip stayed in the East and that he didn't come back home from Tokyo until 1946. In Basil Boothroyd's book, Prince Philip, An informal Biography, published in 1971 it is written down that the HMS Whelp harbored in the Bay of Tokyo on September 2nd 1945 when the Japanese capitulated. Shortly after, Japanese generals handed over their swords to the Allied Commander Lord Mountbatten, Prince Philip's uncle. And he decided to use the HMS Whelp to bring war detainees back home before returning to Portsmouth, the port of registry. In one sentence the author mentions that the HMS Whelp was off duty. Whatever this is supposed to mean. «

» Well, then, 1:0 for the claim, Prince Philip was in South Asia when you were conceived and it would have been relatively difficult to come to Germany in order to conceive you with your mother?« Arthur said with a sheepish grin on his face.
I continued: » Heinz Cramer describes in his book of 1956, Elizabeth II that Uncle Mountbatten and his nephew Prince Philip came together on the evening of the Japanese truce signing in September 1945. Mountbatten is cited to have been talking to Philip about his overseas engagement and that it was about time for him to return back to England. Upon hearing this, Philip stormed to the telegram station shouting to the radio officer's station: Private telegram to London, please! A few hours later a telegram for Princess Elizabeth is supposed to have arrived at the post station of Buckingham Palace with the message: Hope to be in England soon. With best wishes, Philip. «

» But that is not all, «, I added, » in Louis Wulff´s book, Elizabeth and Philip, published 1947, Philip is described as returning to England in 1945 wearing a beard and being asked by Elizabeth to shave it off. «

» 1:1 «, Mill said laughing at Arthur.

» This text passage with the beard now «, I said, » is of great importance for the fact that the picture my mother gave me showed Prince Philip with a beard. Witnesses of that time can still prove this. I found this picture again in Brandreth´s work and was of course extremely surprised to find this picture once more. Next to the text it says that this picture was Elizabeth's favorite picture during the war. If she had known that I, as a child, also held this picture like that in my hands. «

» Günther, you really are terrible at times and not very charming! « Arthur warned.

»Senor Focke, you still must have been very little when you got the picture from your mother. How can you tell that it was really him? «, asked Miguel.
» I am an Eidetiker! «, I answered, not sure of the English word.

» A what, if you don't mind me asking? «, he replied.

» He means that he has a photographic memory «, Mill explained.

» Correct. You should also not overlook the fact that this picture and the testimonies of my aunt and Heiner Kleinert identify him as such «, I pointed out.

»Please let me, dear Günther Focke, play the role of Advocatus Diaboli. All these testimonies are based on memories. It is also known that collective false memories exist. How would you contradict this skepticism here? «, - Miguel asked.

» You see, Miguel, as a detective I can only put together a puzzle. My attention has to focus on the fact that all the single parts draw a logical picture. I have never claimed that I had a single piece of undeniable evidence ...«

Arthur suddenly cut me off: » You can be very diplomatic, Günther. Where do you get this from? First you make a lot of noise and then you revert to playing subtle moves? «

» Arthur please ... I was about to say, that ... « - I lost it for a moment. » that all the parts together have to draw a logical picture. And by following my methodical way, I first had to check if what the Palace says can actually be true. «
» What exactly was the methodical way, dear Günther Focke? «, Miguel asked.

» I contacted the Navy Ministry and asked for the log books of the HMS Whelp. These log books give every detail of what happens on the ship, even when an officer leaves and comes back on board. But, surprise, surprise! Someone must have performed an act of magic! All the log books of the HMS Whelp had disappeared, they were – as they said, not stored. This means that it is not possible to really prove if and when Prince Philip was on board of HMS Whelp. Documents of different ports about arrival and departure dates of the HMS Whelp, however, show that he had already arrived in Portsmouth in January 1946. This is assuming he was on board the HMS Whelp. When I followed the ship movements during the time in question, I wondered why neither arrival nor departure dates of the ships were registered. It is impossible that such a ship was not registered. The ships needed to be reloaded again with ammunition, repairs had to be carried out and it had to be refueled. In short, preparations had to be made for their next military mission.

I found it interesting that HMS Whelp left Tokyo on September 9th 1945. It arrived in Hong Kong on September 13th and on December 6th it left Sydney. The date of when they arrived in Sydney cannot be found in the documents.

The ship could theoretically have left the port of Hong Kong the same day it arrived there and would have been at sea literally anywhere until December 6th, leaving a blank spot of it's whereabouts from September 13th to December 6th. For eleven weeks the HMS Whelp was nowhere.

The Spaniard piped up: » Do you want to imply that this gap means that the HMS Whelp could have traveled to the German North Sea coast and back in eleven weeks only to make it sound plausible that Prince Philip could have been responsible for conceiving you in October 1945? «

» No « I replied, » It appeared to be more plausible for the speculation that he left Hong Kong towards Europe by plane, because Hong Kong back then was a colony of the crown and there were definitely flights to Europe. And, as we know, he also went back to Europe during the war and this was certainly not by sea. He could have easily traveled from Hong Kong to Europe. You know, it was clear that all this was mere speculation. Maybe it would have made more sense, I thought, to contact his former companion and friend Michael Parker. I did so. He did get someone to reply to me by fax, saying that he was otherwise busy at the time and his assistant was not allowed to give out any information. «
»What happened to Parker anyway, Günther? «, Arthur asked.

» Being an intimate friend of Prince Philip, he became private secretary. I think in 2001 he passed away well over 80 years of age. «

» After this investigation, Günther, you can take for granted that the Palace cannot prove that Prince Philip was in Melbourne «, said Mill, » And, it's absurd to presume that all the log books of the HMS Whelp simply disappear. One could pretend that his very influential uncle, Mountbatten, took care of deleting these log books. My tendency would be to put you in the lead by 2:1 now. «

» If you do sports, do not forget that any sport achievement gets documented. Our dear friend didn't really achieve anything in this field «, Arthur added, pushing his way in, » At least nothing positive in his favor. It feels like you want to take the victory only because the statements of the opposite side cannot be proved. «

» Mill «, I said, » Even more has disappeared. «

» Günther, should I call a doctor? «, Arthur started to make fun of me.

»Senor, leave him alone, we haven't even seen the tip of the iceberg yet «, Miguel defended me.

» You remember that I mentioned the interview with Prince Philip saying that he was still in Melbourne in autumn 1945? And this 'live' on BBC. I desperately wanted this video footage.

A lot of effort was necessary in order to obtain this tape. However, I made two copies of it, one for me and the other for sending out. I stored the original with a very good friend's of mine. Surely you understand that I don't want to reveal his name. Anyway, I sent one copy to a film production company. My own copy disappeared from my house, so I immediately went to my friend's house in order to get the original, but it was gone, too. The other copy I had sent to the film production company came back some time later as a censored and cut version. Some of what Prince Philip had said had been cut out of context and was newly edited. «

» Don't be mad at me, my beloved one, but I often get the feeling that you are looking for wind mills to prove that there is something producing wind. Where is your squire? «, - and Miguel handed me a cigar.

Reverend Mill laughed.

Arthur thrust himself into the conversation: » Leave him alone, Senor Xavier, please believe me, Günther is the one of the most decent people on this planet; sometimes he is even too decent. If you had seen pictures from his youth and compared them with the ones of Prince Charles, you would not have seen any difference. And you may rest assured that he is too naive to take advantage of his situation, as he sometimes even makes fun of himself by not making anything from this allegation. He is very diligent about his investigative work. It has happened to me before … I once employed Günther to uncover some information and in the end he uncovered much more than I wanted to know, or let's say: more than actually needed to be known

Then it may occur that you have to step up to your client with a strange feeling when he poses the question: I thought you, Sir Arthur, were my lawyer. But let's keep that out. Coming to the point now, I just wanted to say that Günther is really OK, sometimes a little strange with a little chaotic touch, but the longer you know him the more you absolutely appreciate him as a man as well as a detective. Thank God there are not more of his kind. I would have to close my chambers «.
» Tell me, Senor Focke, I love stories, why don't you go ahead and tell us a story in your life as a detective? «, Miguel was curious to know.

» The one with the bomb, back then, in Germany! «, Mill threw in fast.

» Come on Mill, always the one with the bomb! «, Arthur replied, » I would rather prefer the one with the little girl and the man. «

» Sorry, Senor, have you also worked in Germany? « Miguel asked.

» Yes, of course! I did, for example, an apprenticeship with Wolfgang Xanke at the age of 16. He has been an established private detective in Germany for decades. Then, at the end of the sixties I moved to England, also on behalf of Xanke and as a private detective I was able to meet our dear friend Arthur through his network. «

» Günther, you don't have to go into detail about that now. We are very close, but this goes too far now. «, Arthur interrupted in a very obvious and energetic way.

Maybe he was right and now was really a good moment to ease the tension in the discussion with a crime story. Of course we were just amongst ourselves, a small Gentleman's Club and with Arthur's authority we were bound together like brothers. You could imagine we were a little private club or even a lounge club. Still, I always knew that Arthur played a game and had other intentions with us, maybe also with me, that I could not even think of. I did not understand why he now wanted to keep quiet about how we got in contact with each other, how he met me through middlemen of Xanke's network and how he was always checking my integrity with strange and partly made up or artificial scenarios. But one of my strange characteristics is to be able to wait and not to show all my cards at once. So I started to tell about the story of the lost girl and the man.

» This case took place in Germany in 1968. My girlfriend back then, Brigitte, woke me up one morning shaking me, - something unusual, because normally it is her who took ages to be woken up. She shouted: » Günther, Günther, wake up! The office wants to see you! « Luckily she had already prepared a coffee for me.

This was the last day of my vacation. So, something of great importance must have occurred. I had a sip of coffee and made my way straight to Xanke.

Xanke came right up to me as I entered the office.

» We have an assignment. We have to find a girl who has disappeared. «

Xanke's voice and tone sounded pretty concerned and pressing. » The background, my dear Günther, is as follows: A very young girl from a wealthy family has fallen in love with this American and he allegedly holds her hostage against her will. The American is stationed in Bremerhaven. His name is Sam Mulligan! «, Xanke informed me.

» Are there any other links? «, I asked him, » or any hints? «

» No, this is all we have. You can do it. I have total trust in you. Act like you are under time pressure and she was your own daughter! «

I must admit, I had never seen Xanke show such emotion. Normally he led his life in the serious and methodical way reflected in his work. It became a part of him; he was calm, thoughtful and had an analytical view on each case, just as he handled all other things in life.

I said good-bye and made my way to a busy (as it was in those days) U.S. night club and asked for Mulligan. They told me, among other things, that Sam Mulligan was a black belt in Karate and was pretty active in this sport. I didn't understand what he really meant by » pretty active «. I asked another GI who told me that Mulligan was under arrest.

This was bad - in many ways. On the one hand it could mean that the girl is locked up somewhere by herself. On the other hand it meant it would be more difficult to make contact with him.
Back then the U.S bases in Bremerhaven were regarded as a sovereign state within the state, making it pretty difficult to get any information and statements.

All I needed now was an idea of how I could get in contact with Mulligan. Clark Poler crossed my mind, so I gave him a call.

» Clark, could you please do my a favor? «

» Yes, Günther, how can I help you, what happened? «

»I have a problem I need to talk to a GI on the base, but he is under arrest. Could you get in contact with him and prepare him for a visit from a private detective? Tell him that it has nothing to do with a police investigation! Also, he can not know that you are Military Criminal Police. «

» Hmm «, Clark grunted. » And how do you want to talk to him? Nobody can get in there and nobody can get out of there! «, he replied.

» I will tell you later about how I am going to actually solve this problem «, I said

Right on the next day Clark called me and reported that he was able to get in contact with Mulligan and that he had prepared him for my visit exactly the way I wanted it to be. Mulligan now knew that I had the intention to talk to him about his girlfriend.

» But Günther! How will you get on base? «, Clark asked me on the phone.

» Let's talk about it in our bar. What about in an hour? «

» Yes ok, Günther! «

When we met, he wanted to know exactly what I intended to do to get on base.

» With you, of course! « I answered harshly. He looked at me slightly flabbergasted.

» With me? «, he said with a compassionate smile on his face.

»Yes, indeed, you smuggle me on base in your trunk! «, I suggested.

»How? Are you crazy? What do you think they will do to us if they catch us? «

»Yes «, I answered, » they will throw us in jail! «

Clark took a deep sip of his coffee cup. I handed him an open Lux cigarette box, knowing well enough he didn't smoke. It was only supposed to be a friendly gesture and to show that I acknowledged his doubts. Although I have to confess, I didn't really take his doubts that seriously.

I was only focused on talking to Mulligan, because I was worried about the girl. The consequences of smuggling civilians onto a US military base in Germany did not really matter to me as I only wanted to speak to this Mulligan. I thought that he could still be under arrest for another week and the girl would maybe die of thirst or that something else could happen to her.

Clark and I chose a day and time when there was not a lot of Military Police on base. I lay down in the trunk of his car. He drove a Ford Mustang. A very elegant and big coupe which had lots of space in the trunk equipped with a light I could turn on and thus was not sitting totally in the dark.

Before Clark closed the trunk he took a last look at me, shaking his head as if to say that I would be a special case of my own. The journey started and we arrived at the checkpoint of the base after about half an hour. The trunk stank of fuel and I had problems to hold back a cough. I could barely hear the conversation between the guard and Clark. I tried to hold my breath as one would say in this case.

The car continued driving. Then it stopped. A door was opened and I heard a key near the trunk. Clark appeared. He pointed to a direction and said: » He is in there! «

I crawled out of the trunk and told him to leave.

» Are you sure? «, he asked me. » Yes, of course «, I replied, » If I get into trouble I know how to get myself out of this situation! «

Clark furrowed his brows looking at me in a concerned way and drove back to the checkpoint.

I quickly entered the building which he had pointed at und moved around the house as if I had known it all my life. I was very nervous, because theoretically they could do to me whatever they wanted to for being an unauthorized intruder inside the security area of a military base. It was 1968 and the general mood within the Military was very agitated because of the Cold War.

Inside the building I asked the first soldier I ran into about Mulligan. I acted as if I were a harmless postman.

Luckily this soldier already knew about a civilian who wanted to talk to Mulligan about his girlfriend. This was my luck – for now.

He brought me to Mulligan's room. I was able to talk to Mulligan for nearly an hour. I told him that he was being accused of having kidnapped a young girl against her will and I explained the consequences this would have, especially if something happened to the girl. Mulligan seemed to be intelligent and understanding. He said, and I believed him, that Elke was with him voluntarily and he gave me the address where exactly I would be able to find her. Of course I had to find out if she is really there voluntarily and not against her will, so I said good bye, thanked him for his friendly collaboration and left.

Standing in the hallway I thought about the best way how I could get out of there. Okay. So I tried to adopt a relaxed and cool pose, just as GI's were known to have throughout the world. My pose was however a little too rigid. Maybe I needed some chewing gum. It didn't matter, I thought, and walked out of this building towards the direction of the checkpoint. I pretended to be as cool as a cucumber. My chances to leave the base without problems were high, because I knew that they only made random checks with people walking out of the base as they were already checked and identified as military personnel when walking in.

» Stop! « a voice shouted from behind. For a second I hoped that this person did not mean me.

» What are you doing here? I know you, you are German! «, the voice said. I turned around with the most harmless view possible on my face. Stepping up to me he said very aggressively: » You are under arrest! «

After all that, they did get me. He brought me to the Military Police office which was in the same building as the checkpoint. I was able to see the guard at the gate from there. He explained to the responsible police officer that I was an "imposter". This is someone who acts like he is part of the set-up.

The doors closed.

» Sit down there! « The officer pointed to a bench. I sat down correctly, closed my thighs and posed my folded hands in my lap. I looked around pretending not to know what was going on.

» Do you have any ID on you? «, the officer asked in a very unfriendly voice. So I handed it to him. »What are you doing here on base? «, he asked determinedly.

» Well «, I said as relaxed as possible, » I was searching for somebody! «

» You were searching for somebody? Well, that is nice of you. We are always happy if someone visits us here and asks for somebody. And who were you looking for? «, he wanted to know.
» I was looking for ... Alex Crusoe! «

A white lie, but this name belonged to someone I have met before in a different case and was very sure he had not made a career in the American Army.

» Alex Crusoe? « the officer repeated and looked in his books on the search for this name. He couldn't find him, of course. » There is no Alex Crusoe here! «, he declared.

I was assured that a person with this name must exist here because I am a private detective, I said, and they told me that I would find him here.

» But first tell me how you got in here! «, he asked angrily.

» I just walked in here «, I explained. Naturally I was afraid that somebody might have seen Clark letting me out of his Ford Mustang's trunk.

» So you just walked in here? «, he asked me not really believing me.

» Yes, indeed. I just walked through the checkpoint and the guard there let me pass « - I pointed to the guard outside who I was able to see through the window of the Military Police office. Why don't you go ahead and ask him. He will recognize me for sure! «

Nothing but lies.

They called the guard who was so surprised by this situation the only thing he could reply was that he could not really remember.

His answer even sounded strange to him probably because he didn't really want to admit that he must have had lost sight of me - or let me enter the base illegally.
Now the officer went into the offensive and asked:

» Can you prove that you really are a private detective and no hostile agent? «

» Yes, of course I can prove it. Please call William Hayle; he knows me and will confirm to you, that « – I greatly played all my cards – » I don't lie! «

This was of course a sophisticated little trick. Finding out that I was really a private detective would not imply that I was still lying about the reason and motive of my visit to the base, but that as a matter of fact I entered the base illegally.

So Hayle was called and - as expected – Hayle confirmed my identity as private detective. In addition to that he said that I work for Wolfgang Xanke. This answer obviously proved that I was no foreign agent. I was made to be 'not guilty' straight away. But still the officer looked at me in disbelief and left the office. I was able to watch him through the office window talking to somebody on the phone. Then he came back and said, » Well let's say you were lucky. I don't even want to know about this Alex Crusoe. And maybe it's for your own good that he is not on this base any more. « He gave the guard a signal and said good-bye.

When the guard accompanied me through the gate the unfriendly civilian Guard, who recognized me at the beginning saw me and said: » Never try to come back here! «

I did not really care about his unfriendliness. He did not know how important it was that I broke into this base.

Back home I called Clark and told him about my short arrest and how I got free again.

» Günther, you have more luck than gallons fit in my Ford Mustang «, he added all happy, » but the truth is we were both were lucky. I hope you will find this girl soon. «

The next day I drove to the address which Mulligan had given me in my search for the girl "Elke".

I rang the bell of the house. A man opened the door. He crossed his very muscular looking arms in front of his chest and stared at me like a farmer looks at a calf lying on a slaughter table. I remained all cool.

» I talked to Mulligan. He explicitly wants me to talk to Elke. It is important. Do you understand that, mate? «

» Well, you must then be the detective. Yes, I understand. Mulligan has already announced your visit. But unfortunately she ran away. «, he said

» Why did Elke, as you said, run away? Did she run away because she knew I was coming or because she had other reasons?

You just clearly said that she ran away and did not simply leave here. What is she scared of? «, I now insisted in a very direct way.

» You know, I don't even know this girl well, so how should I know from what she ran away. Maybe she just left and might come back tomorrow «, he smiled back.

» Ok. I understand. Have a nice day then «, I concluded.

Of course, I did not believe a word he said. His whole attitude along with his tone was adapted in order to defend himself. But why did he respond defensively, I asked myself. If he knew I was coming and Mulligan informed him he should have acted more politely. Or did he have other plans Mulligan did not know about.

I decided to observe the house. But before doing that I needed to get some more information about Mulligan and this house.

At the American bar I was able to find someone who knew Mulligan very well, also because both had attended the Karate club here. His name was Helmut. I ordered an Alster. He told me about knowing this girl Elke. After some time he became pretty talkative, so I had another Alster. And he continued saying that it looked like Elke was hiding somewhere else and definitely didn't want to go back to her parent's house who did not accept the relationship between her and Mulligan.

» I completely understand her point of view, but I still have to convince myself that she acted according to her own will.

We should bear in mind that her parents could tell the police that Elke is missing and blame it on an alleged kidnapping, which would surely make the situation for Elke and Mulligan worse«, I explained to Helmut.

Helmut understood me. He wrote down two addresses and said, » Günther, try here, maybe you get lucky, but it will definitely help you to get further in this case. And I would like to add that there are a lot of evil men around who would like to keep a little Elke in their attic. Don't lose any time and good luck! «

I left, now very worried by what he had to say. Immediately, my thoughts went back to that man at the address Mulligan had given me. It was only a prejudice, of course. In reality there were only prejudices and no real judgments because this whole situation was full of confusion.

The next day I drove to the first address and asked to see Elke, pretending I was an old friend of hers. They denied that I should know her. So I drove to the second address he gave me. A young lady opened the door; she was about 25 years old. Her hair was long and dark

» Good afternoon, my name is Günther Focke, could I just have a few words with Elke, please? «, I introduced myself to her.

» Oh, yes, I know Elke, but I haven't seen her for a few weeks now! «

» Can I leave a message for her? «, I asked gently.

» Yes, of course, you can, please come inside «, she answered, » but I have to admit that I do not know if and when she will be back.

She is having a hard time with her mother at the moment! «

She pointed to a desk. I took a piece a paper and wrote down: Dear Elke, in order to hinder your mum going to the police I need a sign of life. You don't have to be worried. Best regards. Günther Focke, private detective.
I added a business card and asked the young lady: »Excuse me, and what is your name? «

» Johanna! «, she answered.

» Johanna, I will add another business card of mine. If you hear something from Elke, please call me no matter what time! «

We said good bye and I left. I was in a hurry to begin surveillance of that man's house. I decided to sit down near the house dressed like a homeless person. The next morning I drove over to this house in my planned outfit. I sat down on the sidewalk close to the house and tied a blanket around me. It was autumn now and it was already quite cold to sit on a sidewalk.

So I just sat there, lit a Lux cigarette and observed the house. Damn, it was difficult to sit there for hours in the cold and to wait. Nothing happened. On the second day again nothing happened and I thought that all this observation work in this uncomfortable situation was leading nowhere. Then at around 15:00 the following occurred:

A girl matching the description of Elke walked into the house.

I was not really sure if it was her and thought about ringing the bell of the house again. But I thought if the man opened the door again and recognized me in this dress he would know that the house is under observation. Not knowing how he would react I decided to give Xanke a call. .

I went to a public phone booth and called Xanke telling him he should come to this address and ring the bell so I wouldn't have to reveal myself. When I gave him the address he said to my surprise:

» Oh, I know this address; the house belongs to a friend of mine. Okay I am on my way. «

I was a little perplexed to be honest. What would this mean that the manager of the Xanke detective office had close ties to the owner of the house I was observing? Was he somehow involved in this case? And what was this man with the impressive arms doing there?

I was confused for a moment. But before I would make any further speculations I decided to sit down again at my observation post and to wait.

Then I saw Xanke going into the house with a woman who was about 40-years old. After some time they walked back out and were followed by this girl who in fact was Elke. They all walked past me on the sidewalk and the woman pointed to me and said: » What is this man doing there? « Xanke answered: » Sometimes its people like that who find lost little girls! «

In fact, Elke really was with Mulligan of her free will. I don't know whether the family did tolerate this young love afterwards or not, I couldn't say. The reason for Xanke knowing the owner of this house was that she was good friends with Xanke´s ex-wife, as I found out later. But the mother of Elke had nothing to do with the owner of this house or with Xanke. It was a pure coincidence that the manager of Wolfgang Xanke´s detective office was familiar with this address. «

» Ah, I applaud, you are very diligent «, Miguel said, » But also brave, verging on the daring! In addition you were extremely lucky, of course. Why don't you go ahead and tell us the story about the bomb? «

» A very good idea! «, - according to Mill, » I already heard this one a couple of times, but it has fascinated me again and again. «

» And I will go to the balcony, in the meantime, to catch some fresh air. I am also curious to know what Marian has prepared for dinner. Please excuse me! «, Arthur stood up, buttoned up his Cashmere waistcoat, took his cane and walked towards the entrance hall. While he was walking I noticed that he was limping with his left foot more than before.

Meanwhile Mill stood up and refilled our glasses with some more fresh water. Miguel also stood up for a second, went over to the large gothic castle windows, stretched himself while looking through the mosaic window. » Ah «, he noticed, » it's snowing more and more. I wouldn't like to be out there now.

The sun will go down in a few minutes. « He sat back down again and turned to me, » Günther how long have you known Sir Arthur White? «

» Since the end of the seventies, if I remember correctly. I had already been in England for almost ten years back then, but why do you ask, Miguel? « I was curious to know.

» At the end, do you think you have a good relationship, what I mean is a friendly relationship with him? «, he asked in a quite a low voice, as if he feared to be heard by someone. Mill was standing about 20 meters away from us and with his glass of water in his hand he was looking at the patterns on the wall.

I looked at him. What did he want to get at with this question? I didn't know Miguel well enough to talk to him about my doubts I had about Arthur. With Mill it wouldn't be a problem. He really did not see the bad side in anyone. If you told Mill about a crime, including cruel ones, he would be astonished, shake his head and look surprised but in a way as if you had told a person in the ancient world about the technical achievements of the 20th century. He would then lift his brow, » Really, oh my God! How bad is this? «, he then used to say and, shortly after that he would maybe talk about a visit to the museum for example.

» Miguel what would you like to hear? , I asked him directly, » Arthur is a member of several clubs, orders and fraternities and during the Cold War he worked for the military protection service. «

» I know, Günther, excuse me, but my intention is not to sound you out about our friend Arthur, but don't you think it was strange how strongly he refused to talk about a plot against you. Twice he repeated that he would have preferred not to know certain kinds of things concerning you. At first I thought it was a joke. But then it appeared to me he personally would prefer, if ... - how should I put this now, certain things, maybe even illegal things, should not be mentioned. You know, this surprises me for different reasons. First, you have known each other for such a long time. This means he should be well informed about your case. Secondly, he is a cosmopolitan for whom it should not be a problem to speculate in a private circle about certain things. And the third point is that we are, as I thought, in an intimate circle. Where else would you be able to articulate yourself? So why did he try to avoid talking about the inner truth of your case provided there is one? Or is he just playing jokes on you in order to aggravate you a little? «

» I have to show you my respect, you are a good analyst «, I replied, » and I have to tell you with all sincerity that I sometimes asked myself if Arthur was only annoyed and therefore had a go at me, or maybe he knew things which would turn out to be uncomfortable for me in one way or another.

Or maybe it could turn out uncomfortable for him or for us both in the end?

Could it be possible that in connection with my case certain issues are still left hanging in the air and if his name was mentioned then it would lead to acts or statements which would prove to be extremely sensitive? «

Miguel Xavier had put his chin on his hand slightly scratching his three-day beard growth, confused and pointing his lips totally lost in thoughts, staring into the room.

» Hmm ...«, I said.

» Maybe you have already had some signs, be that from the Palace or from within your own close surroundings, that you have an unofficial right, that you are acknowledged, but also have been requested to – and this surely being thought through thoroughly, that you should not go public with what you have heard?«
And he looked me straight into the eyes with his deep dark, gaze, that for a moment I thought that he was talking about himself being a messenger of the Palace.

» Günther, I would like to give you an example of my world. As you know I represent different groups and also private persons in financial trading at the stock markets around the globe. Before I decide to acquire shares, derivatives or whatever I might trade, I have to, of course, very precisely think about what I acquire and why. But not only that - in front of my clients I then need to have explanations why I traded these stocks in that way and not in a different way. And I also need these explanations or arguments in case something goes wrong.

It is all about communication and language. And you know what? In most cases I act on instinct totally independent from what I know of these stocks. But, of course, I can't tell anybody about it. They would crucify me, do you understand? Language and behavior are such complex and highly differentiated matters that you have to consider every little detail.

And maybe there really is a detail lying in front of you that you haven't recognized yet as such. Hold on, isn't there a phrase in German similar to: Whoever looks far away to find the truth and longs for his salvation, has already forgotten about a place where he can find shelter… and how does it end? I think something like: …that rescues him from the storm? «

» I think I know what you mean, Miguel, I am also used to analyzing circumstances and to logically put together pieces of the puzzle, but in the end inspiration and intuition are necessary. Yes, maybe I have been blinded by my profession and maybe I don't see what is staring me in the face anymore. But, it's not the case that I live on an island all by myself and only have to deal with myself. Of course I also have very close confidants, with whom I discuss my thoughts. Speculating, for me, is part of the search for findings; but in the end the only things I accept are facts «, I explained to him.

Meanwhile, Mill had come back from his walk and he put his hand on my shoulder saying: » Did you know that the term "fact", or in plural "facts", originates from the Latin word "facere", and it means to make and to do?

If I remember correctly it was Lessing who translated the Latin word "factum" into German as "matter of fact". And we always think that a fact represents a matter of reality without any intellectual help from our side. Just because the intellect is human and can possibly err. «

Mill sat down with us, folded his hands over his chest, just like a priest, and smiled at us. Then he asked: » Where did Arthur go? Didn't he run away because of your bomb story? «

» Yes«, I said, » and he wanted to go to the kitchen in order to take a look at what Marian prepared for our dinner «, I answered.

» Oh Marian «, Mill started to sigh all of a sudden.

» What about this Marian? «, Miguel wanted to know.

Looking over to Miguel, I pushed forward my lower lip and stared at the ceiling.

» I understand«, said Miguel, also pushing forward his lower lip following me with his looks to the ceiling.

» Günther, don't you feel like telling us the story about the bomb at last? «, now Mill addressed me and seemed to be a little alerted by Miguel's »I understand «.

» Yes Mill, I don't mind, so I started to narrate:

» This case took place at a time which was marked by street protests of the student movement APO and its militant groups, as the Rote Armee Fraktion (Red Army Fraction) at the end of the sixties. During this nervous inner-political situation the German National Railways received a bomb threat and it was my job to find the person who had planted the bomb.

The police called Xanke in his office asking for me.

This was no wonder because when I was younger I had done an apprenticeship with the German National Railways for two years and knew all about their systems and network. It was Chief Inspector Hermann Schramm of the state police office Wesermünde/Bremerhaven who asked Xanke if I, Günther Focke, had some time for them. So that's why Xanke sent me to Schramm.

So I went over to the police office, registered at the reception and went over to Schramm.

» Good morning Mister Schramm, how can I help you? «, I asked.

» Mister Focke, would you like to have coffee? «

» Well, this is the first good idea I've heard this morning! « I countered.

» Come on, Mister Focke, it is still early in the morning! «

I sat down to his right, added some milk to my coffee and looked at him all full of expectation about what he would confront me with.

» Mister Focke, we know that you know your way around the rail network of the German National

Railways. We have the following problem: we are searching for an unknown person who is blackmailing the National Railways. This person we are after wants half a million Deutsche Marks, if we don't give in – according to his threat - he would attach bombs to the railway network and let them explode. So that's why we thought about you, Mister Focke! «

Quickly I cleared my throat. » Mister Schramm, would you like me to help you in this case? «, I asked him now directly.

» Yes, Mister Focke, in such a special case, of course, someone special is needed, someone who knows about explosives and also about the railway system. We have been investigating this case for a week now and in fact we found a bomb attached to the railways in the area of Stade. «

» May I see everything that was found in connection with this bomb? «, I asked him

Schramm brought me to a different room, but in the same building. The bomb as well as the device for attaching it to the railways was laid out on a table. Interestingly, there were little metal pieces inside the bomb to weigh it down. I thoroughly looked at all the pieces, but without touching them - business as usual.

» One moment, please«, I said, » where exactly did you find this bomb device? «

» In between Stade and Bremen! «

I looked at him saying: » Interesting. «

» Why, what do you mean by that, Mister Focke? «

» There is something on this table that doesn't really fit in here! «

» What are you thinking of? «, he asked insistently.

» Please take a look at this short piece of wire rope. « It was maybe 30cm long and the wire rope was interwoven with hemp.

» Such wiring is mainly used for tying up fishing boats. « I said explaining the importance of this piece of evidence.

So, now I had to find a village that was close to where the bomb was found.

Or, the person who planted the bomb must live pretty close to the coast or a fishing place, where he would have easy access to such rope. You couldn't buy such wire rope in normal shops. This hemp wire was used by sailors in order to tie their fishing boats to the quay. The wire was twisted like a feather with the hemp wrapped around in between the wire. This way you were able to reduce friction and by that minimize metal abrasion.

After I explained this method often used by sailors to Schramm, he said, » Now you will probably also tell us in which area we can find the person who uses such a rope. «

» Well I think we should start in Wremen, then continue with Dorum, Cuxhaven and then up the Elbe river towards north where you can find fishing boats along the coast. «

Schramm seemed to be surprised about this analysis, but tried to hold it back. He looked at me from the side and said, » interesting «.

This » interesting « was repeated a few more times, with his hands stuck in his pockets and walking around the pieces of evidence as he was looking for more important information he himself could come up with and contribute to this case.

A few days later Schramm called me in Xanke´s office and said in a suspiciously calm tone:

» Mister Focke, there is some more to it I have to tell you about! «

» We have recordings of the blackmailer and also a blackmail letter. «

I immediately drove to Schramm's office. When I arrived he welcomed me right away with a cup of coffee. The tape was sitting on the table. I lit a Lux filter cigarette. Schramm was looking at me waiting for me to be ready for it. So I sat down on the chair opposite him and listened.

Schramm pressed the play button and a voice was heard coming out of the recorder.

» Here speaks the person who planted the bomb. Leave the money at Buxtehude station at 17:00 «

On this day the police surrounded this part of the Buxtehude train station and observed the whole area. The blackmailer had foreseen this and observed the situation by himself. He didn't show up, of course. A few days later the police received another tape from the blackmailer. Schramm called me again and asked me to come over in order to listen to the blackmailer's words.

I listened to it several times and tried to characterize the sound of his voice. Apparently, he had changed it. I asked myself if our blackmailer had put so much effort into it in order not to be identified as a person, or if he had pretended so as not to reveal where he came from by changing the voice.

After about ten minutes I recognized that the caller spontaneously said the sentence » You can't mess with me «. He sounded pretty upset about the investigation work of the police and their game to gain time. The tone of his pronunciation reminded me of somebody who came from Ukraine talking with the same accent - especially when he was very emotional.

I told Schramm: » Our wanted person may come from Ukraine! How many tapes do you have? «

»We have several «, Schramm answered.

» We need a blackboard! «, I jumped off the seat and went over to the anteroom to get a blackboard which was often used by Schramm at briefings.

»Let's write down the preferred times of when this man leaves a message by checking the time of the recorded message. «

We looked over the list and wrote down the times on the board. And now we were able to see that he called in the morning, during lunch time, in the afternoon and in the evening. This only meant that he was either a rich heir or didn't have any work or family obligations.
Since the first possibility was not realistic, we concentrated on searching for a jobless man from the Ukraine.

I asked Schramm if he, apart from the tapes, also had good letters from our wanted person.

» Yes, we do. «, he replied

» Maybe we should copy the blackmail letters and pass them on to the labor offices of the area around Stade, Cuxhaven and along the Elbe estuary, so they can compare the writing with letters of the jobless people. A clerk then maybe recognizes this exact handwriting! «

I was speculating on the chance to find errors in the German handwriting due to the fact that this person may be used to writing Cyrillic letters.

» Great idea! « Schramm said all excited.

After four days a clerk of one of the labor offices said he recognized this exact handwriting. It belonged to somebody from Ukraine. Having observation of the area of the money handover as the only option included the risk of maybe losing the perpetrator with the money, but now the police had the comfortable advantage of being able to observe the potential blackmailer directly.

The police started their surveillance of the now known blackmailer. When a new place and time was arranged for the money handover the police followed him from home to where the money had been placed. They then caught him while he was picking up the money. He called himself McCormic according to the crime books of detective McCormic.

Miguel applauded: Ah! Focke! You will see that other detectives will adopt your name too!

» Or you will become famous one day. Maybe they will make a movie about you. «

» Yes, my nephew has already drawn a comic about Günther´s life! «, Mill remembered, » he called the comic Günther's World! Please forgive him, he just turned 12. «

» Indeed, I will be marketed then as an English-German laughing stock and will find myself on picture inserts of chewing gum packs «, I said.

Mill laughed, » Günther, what's up with your humor? Prince Philip also always gets angry when he remarks that the media made a soap opera out of the Royal Family's life! And somehow, as noted on the side, you are part of this set-up, regardless in whatever form this may be.«

» Life is kitsch! You better get used to this. We are all only court jesters in the world of history and to God who probably … must be a woman! «, Arthur explained, who just came back to join us again.

» Arthur «, Mill called, » I hope you have some good news for us! Especially with regards to the food! «

» Yes Mill, I always think of you, - I just came back from Marian, she is having some problems with the electrical system in the kitchen, nothing works. We started to put the frozen food in the courtyard since its cold enough outside. But tonight we will only have some appetizers. And for later on tonight, - looking at me while saying it, I have a little surprise for us. We will have somebody paying us visit.

» A circus with beautiful girls must have got lost in this area and Arthur, as a gentleman invited them over and offered them a place to stay «, Miguel thought out loud, » didn't you, Arthur? «

» Miguel, you didn't know that here in these ruins someone always pays a visit around midnight, did you? «, Mill smiled at us.

» Do you mean ghosts? «, - Miguel asked back.

A creaking and squeaking sound clanged behind us. The two huge folding doors opened uncovering a dark and only slightly lit room behind our hall.

» Marian, this must be Marian with tea and sandwiches! Mill, «, Arthur urged him on with his arm, » why don't you be so kind and go ahead and help her! «

Miguel stood up immediately and said to Mill who obviously had a problem with getting out of the deep leather seat in his black cloak: » I join you, Reverend, please take my hand. It's the one of an honest skeptic! « He pulled Mill out of the chair and both went towards the wide open door.

Arthur was sitting right in front of me. We were now left alone in this room with the open fire. He looked at me through his thick glasses. He leant his arms onto the armrests, folding his hands, » Günther, what exactly did you tell Fiona King back then? «

» Fiona? «, I asked, » why do you mention her now? Yes, she once visited me at home and saw pictures of Philip, Charles and me on the wall. Of course she could see the similarities, so I told her. «

» What do you think, where does she have the phone number of this castle from, Günther? Not even my own wife has it! «

» She called here? Is she our visitor? « I gulped. Fiona. Oh my god, Fiona. I haven't seen her in a long time. She played a key role in a blackmail case, in which Arthur was involved. I was a little bit in love with this beautiful girl. We called each other once in a while. But, how did she know that I was here and where did she get this phone number from?

» Arthur, I don't have a clue where she got this number from. But let me ask you the question of what you know about her? If I remember correctly you didn't really care about who was behind this blackmail case. The only important thing to you was that this blackmail case was solved and that you didn't have to pay anymore. You didn't even know that Fiona was the sister of Sarah who was pregnant back then and you didn't really care about that, did you, Arthur? « My voice cooled down.

» The fact that a lady will visit us will not only compromise the situation for me, because someone will be sitting opposite me in this circle who knows I have an illegitimate child with her sister, but also my dear Focke, because I have to assume that this person who illegitimately has the phone number of this castle also knows other telephone numbers, for example«, - Arthur was almost trembling now, » the one where we last met! «

» Arthur, I always keep my secret numbers in a secure place, including the ones relating to Buckingham Palace. To my knowledge, this phone book got out of my hands only one time.

This was when the police accidentally suspected me of smuggling and arrested me. They raided my house, found this phone book and confiscated it «, I explained to him.
» Well, you never told me about this? «, he replied.

» Arthur! «, I said with emphasis, » that happened a long time ago, forget about it! Back then I didn't know about your meetings in these castles and consequently didn't have any of these phone numbers. With regards to Fiona, let me tell you that she is one of the most wonderful people I have ever met in my life. I can't picture her having found my phone book and copying the numbers out of it. Furthermore, when she was at my place we had an Alster beer and she became so tired that she fell asleep in my arms. I was with her the entire night, Arthur, and she just slept, please believe me. «

Arthur stood up, went over to the chimney, added some pieces of wood, took the burner from the cornice and lit a fire. He then went over to the cabinet, took out five glasses along with a bottle of sherry and tried to fill them up. I said 'not for me'. He filled one of these three times, quickly downing the contents each time.
He leaned against the chimney, looked down to the floor tracing the Paisley pattern of a small carpet with his slippers. » Have I ever told you, Günther, that … «

Then there was a clanging sound. We looked towards the folding door. Mills and Miguel entered the room with two little trolleys with salads and sandwiches on top closely followed by Marian carrying a large silver plate.

» Ay, Hombres «, Miguel proclaimed, » here we go with the food for the gladiators in this madhouse! «

She came up to us and placed the plate on the long and low couch table in the middle of our circle. This plate was covered with small bowls with different dips, olives, pickles and chips. There was something for everybody.

Marian was dressed all in black, sweater, trousers and flat shoes. She also wore a tiny white pinafore and a white bonnet, which reminded us that she was a cook. She was tall and slim, lithe like a ballerina. She was still very attractive, although she must have been over 60 years old. Her dark hair was tied back tightly into a bun. She wore a tight, brown, about 4 cm thick leather band around her neck, which seemed to restrict her neck movements a little.

» Madame «, Miguel uttered, » do you have some chili or hot pepperoni? I'm afraid I finished what I had at the last service station. « He was holding a little pill box in his hand.

» Miguel! «, Mill said, shaking his head.

Arthur handed a sherry glass to every one of us. 'Dear friends he said, I'm happy about coming together with you again. Unfortunately our friend Townsend cannot be with us this time.' Arthur lifted his glass and emptied it. We followed suit.

» Oh, by the way, I have an invitation for all of you to a garden party in Jersey this summer. I will be baptizing one of my sisters' daughters. A real sweet child - her name is Deborah. You are more than welcome to join me. « Mill said, » but I still don't know ... «, he interrupted himself, as he had underestimated the size of the appetizer he had put in his mouth. We waited patiently until he was finished chewing. » ...how we will all get there, so please let me know if you will be attending or not. «

Marian brought in a third trolley with drinks for us. She knew about my fondness for Alster beer. I picked one up and sat back in my chair observing the circle of friends. Mill was enjoying a salmon sandwich, Arthur a huge salad and Miguel was crumbling chili onto his olives. Arthur had a glass of white wine, Mill a light beer and Miguel tried one red wine after the other, but none seemed to be right for him – just like when we had the last meeting. Then he turned to me.

» Günther «, he said, »earlier you explained how you perused books about Prince Philip researching his whereabouts during the time you were conceived. And you mentioned that you had the impression that in all of the books published after 1994 somebody wanted to indirectly communicate with you.

So you tried to read very carefully and in doing so also tried to get to know and to be close to your, as you see him, father. If you think of what your impressions were in these passages, how does Prince Philip appear to you? Do you feel that he and you are similar? - I mean just from reading these excerpts? Do you care at all? Or - in an abstract sort of way - can you see yourself in him, judging by the characteristics he has? «

» But Miguel, what kind of question is that «, Arthur threw in, » Prince Philip grew up in totally different surroundings than Günther. Even when he was young he had a totally different educational and general background. Günther is from Wremen and he had to teach himself almost everything, - and admittedly, it was a lot, whereas Philip grew up in Greece, attending schools in Paris, Germany and England and, up to today, he has felt at home at sea. There is no way you can compare the two. «

» Arthur «, Mill added, » this is exactly the point. What Miguel wants to say is that even though there are these colossal differences, - and if we compare ourselves to Prince Philip we are all nothing but different sized small fish - there is still something like an inner side or identification within oneself that could exist between the two. Just think about the similarities there are in the face of father and son.

» I didn't know much about my father for a long time either, you know what I mean? I was already a young man when my mother finally told me about my father. He didn't raise me, but there are still surprising similarities to our behavior.

» This is called genetic likeness «, Miguel explained.

» Ok then, Günther, start telling us about it«, Arthur requested.

» Arthur, «, I remembered, » it is not as simple as it seems. Of course I read between the lines. I read these books so I could ask myself if there were any matching characteristics. But if I tell you that they write that he is stubborn, well then, Arthur, am I not the same way? Furthermore, he will always contradict and always wants to be right. Don't I do the same at times? I also read about him that he likes to give presents and that he is anxious to take care of everything and everybody. He also feels responsible ... «

» Oh my god! Günther! That is exactly like you! I still remember how you always fought with the DVLA car tax revenue authorities and were more than willing to even protect everyone who had had bad experiences in Corby, because you thought you really had to take care of everything. And you did this in such calmness and hard-headedness, that if you call someone you sometimes ask yourself 'oh no, what is he up to now'«, Arthur declared.

» Oh well «, I said.

»Günther, there are times I really don't know if you are crazy or what you are trying to get at with your sense of justice and truth. You don't really see how annoying this can sometimes be for others. Oh Günther, what should we do with you «, he said in a resigned manner.

»Someone should send you an angel! «, Miguel added.

» An orchestra of angels! «, Arthur overruled him.

» Somebody has to do the job. And Günther, however, is radical about his approach to life. Don't you think he knows that he sometimes even argues with the gods about which color the horizon should be? Do you think he enjoys being Günther Focke? Do you think it is funny? What if those closest to him had told him 'there lad, there in this Palace is the one who fathered you'? «, Mill asked slightly upset. » Who is your father, Senor Focke? «, asked Miguel.

» Well the question should be: Who is this husband of Queen Elizabeth II, Queen of England, the one who defends our beliefs, the highest representative and queen of 16 out of a total of 53 Commonwealth countries. «, Arthur added up.

» You know, when Mr. Heiner Kleinert told me in no uncertain terms back then that Prince Philip was my dad, I didn't really like this idea, because of various reasons. And if it was true, that I am, in fact, the premarital son of Prince Philip, Duke of Edinburgh, Baron Greenwich, Earl of Merioneth, husband of the Queen of England and of the Commonwealth, then there would probably never be an official confirmation of where I come from. Even worse: My existence would represent an affront towards the British Royal Family. Well, even the claim; or let's better say: even the speculation would be beyond common sense.

There were times when I really thought whether it would not have been better if he were a band leader from Liverpool - a small galaxy below the family of the British Empire's highest representative - the soul of Great Britain. Really, I often felt miserable.

I already heard people laughing at me, if I would even dare to vaguely suggest my origin. And the media! Don't forget about the media, how they would fight like dogs for this little piece of scrap meat with the initials G.F.! Not because of me, but just to declassify this mystical aura surrounding the royal house down to a profane, even down to a human institution, while they ... But let's leave that aside.

Often I experienced a certain kind of solidarity towards my alleged father who avoided, ignored and only appeased all press releases about his – let's say: secret liaisons and whatever else there was, with a simple "no comment".

Of course it was not my intention to willingly destroy what I had just discovered and perhaps also had discovered by good fortune, by trying to snatch it and to name him by his real name.
But just thinking about my origin does not simply end at that point, just because I started to think about myself «.

» Günther, of course not, Günther Focke, you see yourself in the mirror the next and each following day, posing yourself the same question over and over again. You can't escape from it. It turns into being your psychodrama. A stigma within yourself«, - Mill explained.

» You know, Mill, I would have loved to forget about the question. But forgetting about it all would only be possible if I had the chance to get a definite answer. So this is what I looked for. How else would I have been able to confirm or deny it? And believe me, at the end I didn't care about the results. The main point is that the question gets answered and no longer lingers like a wound that will not heal.

» What a paradox. In order to get rid of a question, you normally get more and more involved, and in the end you recognize that there is no end. So you don't see anything and you stay blind. Senor Focke, because of that I take my hat off to you «, Miguel admired.

» Yes «, Arthur confirmed.

» I tried to encourage myself. I lived with arguments motivating me to continue not knowing if I might reach my goals ...

» Stubbornness, here we go again! «, Arthur said.

» How, my friend Arthur, would you react if you were me? Shouldn't I be allowed to ask myself, from where and from whom I come? Why all this mystery? Good Lord! We're living in the 21st century and not even a whiskey maker from Nairnshire would assume that here and there a man has his weaknesses that even a king could feel the desire to be with someone whom he is not betrothed to.

I often weighed up whether I should proceed, being aware that this could cause a great deal of irritation – or to stay silent forever.

But what should I keep silent about? I would happily remain silent, if I knew exactly what to be silent about. You can keep silent about what you know, a fact, but can you also keep silent about something for which there is no answer? «

» Günther, you are right with that. Questions, especially those kinds, are questions you cannot get rid of. But you should be aware of the significance the answer could have for you «, Mill pointed out.

» Mill, it is not about some kind of question, such as 'Does God exist?'. Or 'Does life really come from the sea?'. The question points directly at me personally. At the reason and the origin of my existence and my individuality. The answer to this question cannot be found in just myself, unless I was the one who conceived myself «, I explained.

Miguel joined in by saying, » I understand, Günther, for you it is as if you had to deny this question about yourself, if they did not allow you to research where you originate from. It is like a law of common sense. Do you understand, Mill? «

» It is hidden within ourselves and that is the justification to search for yourself. The reason why you come from somewhere is in your own reflection, yes, I understand and you don't want to just speculate about it! «, Mill said, » It would shift the question into infinity and who would want to bear this pain?

» Exactly Mill «, I added, » Speculation is an uncomfortable fate. Perhaps - I thought pragmatically - I could prove that this alleged noble origin did not exist in order to get rid of this somewhat crazy notion of where I originated from. Then I would finally find peace within myself. I could be a normal man again, without any royal blood; I could repair televisions again, go to sunny places with Rachel and get annoyed about the neighbor's children putting dents into one of my garage doors in Corby, in short: I would be free. «

» Who is Rachel? «, Miguel asked.

» I will let you know some other time «, Arthur answered.

» Well, I understand «, Miguel said.

» What should I do? I relied on my detective work that learned from Xanke. All I needed to do was to be radical in my search for evidence and not just look for indications that there would not be an answer to, such as: 'He is my father'.

First we had to check if Prince Philip could have been in Wremen at this time in question. I got a list of publications about Prince Philip. This list consisted of 56 pages. I only picked out the publications which covered his whereabouts when I was conceived and the ones which could bring me close to him as a man and as a person.

Days, or even weeks I read up about him and I could not stop being astounded. Above all, I was astounded because of the endless branching out of his family tree.

I picked up a book which mainly focused on Prince Philip and his relationship with Elizabeth in search of clues in there that were worthwhile pursuing. I skipped a few chapters, was reading criss-cross, and looked at Prince Philip's family tree «.

»Oh, that's very interesting, Miguel, do you know his family tree? «, Arthur asked him.

» I am afraid I am not that familiar with it, I have to admit. But I am learning. «, Miguel answered.

So I continued:

» What I did not know at the beginning was that the British Navy officer, Prince Philip, was not an

Englishman, but a Greek - Prince Philip of Greece. Right before his marriage to Elizabeth he became an Englishman. How did that happen?

His father was Prince Andreas of Greece and his mother's name was Alice of Battenberg. His father Andreas had seven brothers and sisters. The father of Andreas, however, was Georg I., King of Greece and married to Grand Princess Olga of Russia.

I further traced the family tree. The parents of George I of Greece were Christian IX, King of Denmark, and Princess Louise of Hessen-Kassel. The parents of his wife, Queen Olga, were Grand Duke Konstantin of Russia and Princess Alexandra of Sachsen-Altenburg.

So, in the end, Prince Philip unites a German-Russian-Danish background, although, in the end he was the Prince of Greece.

Miguel interrupted me: » Why did the Greeks not have their own Head of State? «

Arthur, very knowledgeable of history, explained:

» In 1830 the Greeks were freed from Turkish domination. England, France and Germany appointed Otto of Bavaria, a brother of the famous Prince Regent Luitpold, as Greek Head of State. You laugh, but this is true. It was he who had to tie the freed Greeks to Europe (the Occident), away from the Ottoman Empire. However King Otto was chased away after over 30 years of reign, and the man from Wittelsbach was tired of his long reign in Greece. After him, Prince Wilhelm, the second son of the Danish King Christian IX., was put on the throne in 1863. He named himself Georg I., King of the Hellenes. He kept Otto´s country colors "blue and white". And still today they make up Greek's national flag in horizontal stripes. Unfortunately, King Georg I. was shot dead by a madman. There you go. «

» Please let me to recount, «, Miguel said, » so your paternal grandparents would be Andreas of Greece and Alice of Battenberg and your great-grandparents would be George I. and Olga of Russia. Your great-great-grandparents would then, according to this description, be Christian IX., King of Denmark and his wife Princess Louise … ah, please help me. «

» Louise of Hessen-Kassel «, Mill said.

» Wait, Miguel, it will get even better «, Arthur warned.

» Alice of Battenberg, the alleged paternal grandmother of Günther was the daughter of Princess Victoria of Hessen and Ludwig, Marquess of Milford Haven.

He originated from the morganatic marriage of his father, Prince Alexander of Hessen with a Polish countess. The Grand Duke of Hessen gave her the title, Countess to the Princess of Battenberg. As was commonplace with morganatic marriages that children inherited the title of their mother's family. Their son Ludwig of Battenberg joined the British Army before World War I, after which he was given the title Marquess of Milford Haven.

Princess Victoria on the other hand was the daughter of Princess Alice and the Grand Duke of Hessen. And this Alice was the daughter of that Victoria of England, who was married to Prince Albert of Sachsen-Coburg and Gotha «, Arthur explained.

» Yes, but «, Miguel lifted his forefinger.

» Just a moment, Miguel «, Mill quickly added, « what is interesting is that our Elizabeth II who married Prince Philip, is a great-granddaughter of Victoria, just as Princess Alice of Battenberg is a great-granddaughter of Victoria. » So, one could define Prince Philip and Elizabeth II as cousins «, Miguel concluded.

» Yes, of course, but in a very distant way! «, Mill said.

» The parents of Elizabeth II. were Queen Mother Elizabeth and George VI.. His parents were

Princess Mary von Teck and George V. And in turn her parents were Princess Alexandra of Denmark and Edward VII.

From there you get back to the famous Queen Victoria and Prince Albert of Sachsen-Coburg and Gotha «, I added.

» I have to admit, I am astonished, I really was not aware of all this. I make note of this fact herewith. But how could a Greek man become an English Navy officer and marry an English royal? «, Miguel asked.

» You are forgiven, Miguel «, Arthur said, » Günther may I please continue? Back then it was actually not that easy for Prince Phillip to become an Englishman. It was a sign of the times, not just from a legal point of view.

Because, Miguel, two years after Germany's capitulation and after realizing on what a grand scale the atrocities of the Nazi regime were, nobody of course wanted to see a German next to the commander of the glorious flagship. Some of the conservative Englishmen considered the Greek prince as a German due to his historical origins.

In addition there was another problem. Greece didn't want to let go of their own prince. Please bear in mind how paradox this situation was for Prince Philip. He was a British Naval officer during the war, born as Prince of Greece and inherited the title of his father "Prince of Greece and Denmark". Some Englishmen, though, saw him as a German because his mother's name was Alice of Battenberg «.

» Your situation is and remains a paradox! «, Miguel summed up.

Mill now joined the discussion:

In order to clarify the origin of Prince Philip, a law from the year 1701 was found under the name of "Act of Settlement", which says that the countess Sophie of Hannover and her heirs were the next Protestants in line to the throne in England or Great Britain. In 1706 the following law "Act of Naturalisation" even officially granted Sophie and her heirs English citizenship. As Prince Philip also comes from this bloodline - a fact that was verified by lawyers in England - he was then a British citizen from birth. Furthermore, this law makes the entire German royal family eligible for a British passport. «

» So this means that the entire royal family in Germany are English citizens at the same time? « Miguel wanted to know.

» Exactly – if they can provide proof they are related to the countess«, Arthur said reassuringly.

» Let me explain a little more about how Philip came to his name«, I wanted to add, » because you may ask yourself of how someone who was just recently identified as an Englishman could be called Prince Philip. The family name of his great grandfather, King of Denmark, was Schleswig-Holstein-Sonderburg-Glücksburg. It was difficult to anglicize such a name. The dynasty of Holstein originally came from the Oldenburg dynasty. In English you could rephrase this as Old Castle.

In the end his mother's surname, Alice of Battenberg, was chosen as the new name. However put into English they used Mountbatten instead of Battenberg. This made Philip of Greece to English Lieutenant Philip Mountbatten. «

» Well ok «, Miguel said, » but how did he grow up? «

I continued reporting:

» He had four sisters. His mother Alice of Battenberg was supposed to have been hard of hearing and his father Andreas of Greece was mainly short-sighted. «

» Have you had such problems either? Maybe caused genetically? «, Miguel was curious to know, joking a little.

I turned to Mill: » Reverend, say something! «

» As you wish, Günther! Well in the meantime Alice had spent some time in a mental institution. Her sense for spirituality was supposed to have been slightly exaggerated - whatever this means. Patients in mental institutions were only in the wrong place at the wrong time and that is the reason they were in a mental home« Mill smiled at all of us and continued.

» Alice is supposed to have said once that she was the wife of Christ, when actually she was merely a helpful and caring person. You have to realize that this beautiful, young lady helped out in hospitals during the Balkan war, while Philip's father, Andreas of Greece, lead the Army against the Turks. Obviously they could have lived in the lap of luxury, if they had wanted to.

When the war seemed to be lost, his family fled to relatives in Paris. Princess Marie Bonaparte, a granddaughter of Christian IX., King of Denmark, was a patron of Sigmund Freud in Paris.

And then she sent poor Alice to him, for God's sake. Freud of all people! Apparently, it took her a long time to get better. She is supposed to have always run around in a baggy overcoat. There are pictures, where she stands in front of the Palace dressed as miserable as Mother Theresa. «

» I would like to add something about Prince Philip's education «, I explained, » he went to a private pre-school in Paris. Then he was sent to a boarding school in Cheam, Surrey. In 1933 he transferred to a boarding school in Salem, Germany. Hitler was already a major talking point in Germany at that time. In order to flee the upcoming Nazi regime he left with the director of Salem, Kurt Hahn – an intellectual – to Gordonstoun, until he then registered with the Royal Navy College in Dartmouth. «

» What was he interested in? «, Miguel asked.

» He preferred sports to art. Joining the Navy was the family tradition. But his real love is flying. In 45 years he has spent 6000 hours flying 59 different aircraft. He is a colonel, a regiment leader, a field marshal, an admiral, a major general, a founder, fellow, patron, president, chairman and a member of more than 800 organizations. And besides this he is part and parcel of everything the Royal Court is involved in. Whether I am his son or not, I would already have gone crazy «, I said.

» Well, you are not interested in art either, dear Günther«, Arthur said, » all this is highly interesting, above all, his knowledge and the circles Prince Philip moves in. «

» Yes, up to a certain degree knowledge also means power. But there is also a level of knowledge, when you don't have any power anymore«, Miguel said.

»On the other hand there is a level of power which means you don't find out about certain things; this means things are kept secret for fear of having to suffer the consequences «, Mill added to the conversation.

» Yes, the king is always aware of the fact that a Richelieu thinks he would have all the power and knowledge and through this he would be a leader by fate. But it is exactly this type of fate that protects a king from a Richelieu «, said Arthur.

» Sir Arthur, do you know a Richelieu? «, Miguel asked him.

Arthur smiled in a superior way and said: » forget about it, my friends «, he looked at me, » Günther, you haven't told us how the Christmas tree business was going before Christmas! «

» What? «, Miguel did not understand.

Mill laughed, » Senor, you do not know, of course, that our friend Günther, among others, has a thing for fir trees, driving to Lands End every year to cut hundreds and selling them on a market as a Christmas time. «

»Oh yeah «, I said, » I even had to find a lost girl! «

»Oh my god! Arthur said, » You can't go anywhere by yourself, because wherever you go something happens! «

» But then something would also need to happen today! «, Mill said laughing.

» Let's not underestimate anything, dear Mill «, Arthur warned and lit a cigar again.

» Please tell us the story, dear Günther «, Miguel called upon me.

» Well ok «, I started, » when my friend Andrew and I took off from Corby towards the South, we had very bad weather. We arrived somewhere near the Lands End region in the early afternoon. We got stuck in the mud on the dirt roads again and again. Whenever I jumped out of the Rover it was a leap in the dark. I was afraid to jump into mud next to the alleged track in the moor and to completely sink in for a while. Normally, these things always happen to me. «

» I have always been happy when I made it back home from England «, Miguel interrupted me.

I went ahead, » you have to bear in mind that it gets dark there very early this time of the year. One moment you think you still have enough time to do what you are doing and then, suddenly, you don't see anything anymore. The air is really humid and fog appears so fast as if someone had hung up a curtain so you could not see anymore. You don't see anything anymore and, above all, you don't even hear anything. All of a sudden the sound is absorbed by the humidity, so you lose your orientation straight away. This can lead to wrong or even fatal reactions when you are on the moors.

On the first day now, we had just arrived and Andrew disconnected the caravan from the Rover in order to get it ready for the first night. The lumbermen still weren't there. I got out very carefully and disappeared for a moment behind the bushes. It was already quite crepuscular.

When I was back in the caravan getting ready to sit down, we heard an upset female voice shouting. We looked at each other wondering who the hell could be out in this area at night. Did we maybe confuse it with a blurred sound of an animal?

Andrew looked out of the caravan door and there was this lady standing in front of us, shaking, all wet and wearing dirty clothes.

» My daughter, have you seen my daughter? My little Dorothy, she just turned 14. I cannot find her. I have been running around for at least an hour, but you cannot see anything anymore. «

This lady was completely hysterical. Totally understandable, of course. First of all we took her arm and brought her inside the caravan. Andrew made a hot tea. She embraced the glass with her hands obviously warming herself.
» Could you call the police? «, she asked.

» No, unfortunately not. We left our mobile phones at home, because we don't have any connection out here anyway «, I explained to her, » let's drive to your place. «
I sat her down in the Rover and we drove all the way to her house.

It was not too far to her street, not even a kilometer. There were five or six midsize houses in her neighborhood. I drove through the court gate and stopped in front of the lit up entrance door.

Her husband, Mr. Peterson, was already waiting for her. We called the police in Devon.

Constable Schneckhart answered the phone. » Schneckhart? «, was heard on the other side of the line. I explained to the constable what the situation was and asked him to come here with some police officers.

» Can't you call the police station in Launston or Plymouth? «, he suggested.

I thought I didn't hear right. » But this is at least 200 miles away from here «, I protested.

» I know, but I am here all by myself « he shouted through the phone.

» When will your colleagues come back? «, I asked him.

And he said: » You don't understand, mate. I am always here by myself. «

I saw Mr. Peterson embracing his wife and both looking at me full of worry. Now I started to talk to constable Schneckhart in a more dominant way: » I am pretty sure that the police of Lands End have well trained, brave police officers who carry out their duties at all hours, don't they? Am I wrong? «

» No, well, you are right. Where should I come to? «

» Where should you come to? «, I repeated. Mr. Peterson said: 3 Mary Hill. And I repeated: » Three Mary Hill! «

Schneckhart answered that he was on his way.

I hung up, went to the window and looked outside. It didn't stop raining. » How is your daughter dressed? «, I asked.

» The whole day she was wearing jeans and a skimpy sweater. When I then looked in her wardrobe the only thing missing was a jeans jacket «, she reported.

I sat down with the parents and asked them if they knew where she could have gone. In this area there is nothing except a few houses on Mary Hill and miles of moors, marshes and forests. Civilization starts again near Launston about 20 miles away from here. I gave it a quick thought that I would drive down the road towards Launston. I didn't think that the young girl would hide in the bushes.

» I already went to all the families here in this area. Nobody has seen my little Dorothy! «

» Does your Dorothy have friends here in this area? « I asked her. She shook her head and said there is only Lisbeth. She lives across the street and is all worried, too.

I tried to calm the woman and her husband down.

» Mr. and Mrs. Peterson, there are still a lot of possibilities to find your daughter. Trust me. I have been private detective for decades and I have already found a lot of people who had disappeared. «

The woman looked at me as if nearly paralyzed. Trying to play down the tension I added: » And all were alive when I found them! «

Her husband smiled faintly. »Yes, that is nice, in a city and with time and witnesses maybe, but here? In the dark, with fog and rain, how do you want to find a girl in time around here at this time of the year, before the weather kills her? His wife started to cough.

Remembering that I had a friend not far from hear in Devon I quickly continued: » There is a colleague of mine in Devon. He could equip me with some night vision devices. In the darkness you can recognize even a rabbit at a distance of about 100 meters. «
With this information I was hoping to bring a little hope into this delicate situation. Seriously, I wasn't really confident in finding this girl in time and alive. In this sort of area you will survive for an hour with these clothes. After that your body can't take it anymore and collapses. This humidity soaks the clothes and you feel the cold as the dampness penetrates your skin. It feels like being in ice cold water. In addition the cold humidity in your lungs cools you also down from the inside. I looked at that small family holding each others´ hands and staring into the room. I didn't express my thoughts about this girl which crossed my mind. A nightmare.

On the other hand I thought that it was possible to find her more quickly just because she was dressed in such a light way. She was no careless tourist, who travels in this area for the first time. Maybe somebody picked her up with a car and took her home, so she thought that she would not need warm clothes.

Somebody knocked at the door. Ah, I thought, this must be the lonely and brave police officer. The woman jumped up right away and opened the door. As expected it was police constable Schneckhart. He came in and immediately started to give excuses for his delay, complaining about a construction site which was under water because of the rain, of course. » Constable, it's time for coffee! « It was necessary to calm this situation down a little bit. I had difficulties in thinking straight and now this police officer added fuel to the flames. His behavior was not really productive. In the meantime the lady made coffee. And I lit a cigarette. Forming an 'O' with my lips I slowly and carefully blew the smoke out. Everyone present looked at me full of expectation. I explained to the constable that I had many years experience in such cases as a private detective.

He immediately reacted in a professional sounding tone: »Well yes, I already thought about putting together a search team «

I shook my head. » Constable whom would you find who would be willing to dare his way through the brushwood in danger of being swallowed up by the moor! «

I felt the feeling of fear in Mr. and Mrs. Peterson increase considerably. For a moment the room was totally silent. As I was hoping I still held some aces in my hands.

» Constable, we cannot go out there and look for the girl. We have to carry out an investigation in the classical way. «

» But how? «, the constable asked.

» You know your way around here. Please tell me how many villages are around here in - let's say 30 miles, and what their names are. Then we call the taxi station and all the taxi drivers should receive an exact description of the girl. This way we set up a news network. And because Dorothy is dressed in such a light way, I don't think she planned a night walk through the fields. Is there a pub or a hotel close by here? «

» Yes, of course there is «, Mr. Peterson said.

» Even better! So we can assume that there is still lots of traffic on the streets and that a taxi driver maybe saw her «, I speculated.

Alright then. We called all the taxi stations, telling them about the urgency of this situation and passed on a description of Dorothy. It was almost eleven o'clock at night. Exactly the time when all pubs and restaurants close. So if all the taxi drivers know about it and it takes them an hour from one village to the other and one back we could receive some news within the next two hours.

After that, as I concluded, there would hardly be any taxis driving around and by this the chances to find Dorothy safely would decrease immensely. I tried to think about what we could do if the taxis didn't see Dorothy. What then? Should we still initiate a search operation? Perhaps with the help of the military?

Mrs. Peterson made us another coffee. I kept thinking about my friend Andrew who was waiting for me in the caravan the entire time. I looked at my watch. Only 20 minutes have gone by. In the meantime all the taxi drivers should have got the description from the taxi operator. Either someone will call now or it will be some time between midnight and 1:00am.

So we had coffee. It was a little weak, but strong enough to keep us awake. The constable was telling us some trivial stories in order to relieve his anxiety. Of course, he felt sorry for not really being able to help in this case all by himself. I looked at him and thought, well! But you were known by all the ones you informed in this area and in so doing there was a good chance we would find Dorothy. I also thought about my experiences I had with the police. How often did I have to experience that the police officers didn't want to consider my advice. They must have always been afraid that I would take all the credit. How silly. After all I said what I thought after the police did not know what to do anymore. But this brave little constable didn't have any prejudice against me, so we were able to talk about this case without any power struggle or similar games. The phone rang. Everybody looked at each other.

It took Dorothy's father a second to pick up the phone. » Peterson? « We all looked at him and listened to his voice trying to understand what was said.

His face clearly gave the impression that Dorothy had been sighted and apparently she was fine. He said: » A taxi driver saw her with a guy on a country road near to Morgans. « Schneckhart jumped up and said: » I know where this is, I'll go and pick them up! «

Oh my god, I thought, two young pubescent runaways fearing their parent's punishment and afraid of the weather, both slightly in panic, and then you have Schneckhart approaching them in a police car. So I quickly said: » Let's take my Rover. It is a neutral car. We should bear in mind that the two runaways' might feel guilty, so they would maybe try to hide when they see a police car. «

Schneckhart briefly stopped on his way towards the front door and thought about it. Then he said: » Okay, you are right. Let's take your car. «

I turned to the Petersons and told them: »You both please stay here holding the fort. Anyway we need both backseats for the kids. «

Schneckhart and I took off. I recommended taking a road which made it possible to approach the two from behind. After only ten minutes we saw them. We stopped the car and I opened the window asking: » Dorothy? «

The young girl briefly answered: » Yes! « She then saw Schneckhart´s uniform, so I quickly told her: » Please don't worry. Your parents understand. And they are both happy to welcome both of you back home. «

Dorothy took a quick look at the young man. I leaned over the seat and opened the door. They entered the car not saying a word. We started our way back to her home, 3 Mary Hill. Her mother came outside and embraced her. Right next to them stood her father, a little embarrassed, shaking hands with the young man.

It turned out that Dorothy has already been going out with Tony for six months, but she lacked the courage to tell her parents about it. Furthermore, it was not the first time they secretly met.

I bade farewell and drove back to Andrew. He had already got some Alster beers out.

The next day the Peterson family came over to visit us.

I was very pleased to learn that Mr. Peterson had accepted Dorothy's boyfriend as a family member. We sat together until deep into the night and talked, told stories and laughed a lot. We, that was: Andrew, my little self, Martha Peterson, Sven Peterson, Dorothy Peterson and Tony Watson. It was a lot of fun, although the weather was terrible and my arrival here had started with Dorothy's disappearance.

On the next morning Andrew woke me up by saying, » Günther, the lumbermen have arrived and are already waiting for us. Let's go, let's get some Christmas trees! «
To be honest, I wasn't really in the mood to cut down Christmas trees. But okay. We cut them all down in five days. Many questions crossed my mind during those days. I wanted to be back home soon. What disturbed me the most was that we didn't have a phone and this meant no one could get hold of us. In the last two days luckily the weather improved and the sun came out so we were able to work more effectively. We paid the workers, loaded the lorry with the trees and then finally headed back to Corby. «

» A beautiful story «, Mill said, » it's a good thing that Dorothy's father had accepted the young man. I don't even want to know how many disasters occur just because kids lack the courage to talk to their parents openly. «

» Yes, I confirmed, there must have been an open discussion within the family, because the next day when the Petersons came over, Mr. Peterson said to me: You know, Mr. Focke, back in our days parents didn't have an understanding for such young people holding hands. But times have changed. Today the kids know more than before. And we cannot pretend we're still in the year 1930. «

» What did you answer to that? «, Arthur asked me.

» Well, yes «, I said, » in these days we only complain about moral decay. But the truth is that today morality ranks even higher.

» What do you mean by this? «, Arthur asked.

» I mean «, I tried to explain, » that love and fidelity, understanding and precaution are worthwhile goals and ideals, even today. In our days the punch line was that we followed them not out of constraint and automatism, but out of your own decision and freedom. Is it not an even greater value when you can realize the good out of goodwill and freedom instead out of fearing your parents or socio-political calculus? «

» Whether it's social constraint or not, in the end people should decide for themselves whether they want to act liberally or not, Günther «, Mill added.

» Mill «, I replied, »You see, if everybody prayed to God every evening and went to church every weekend, we then would say this is moral and right. «

» Yes, of course «, Mill confirmed.

» Ah, just a moment please, I know exactly what Senor Focke means to say «, Miguel threw in, » he means that this ritual is actually empty, if your heart doesn't open up to God and instead it becomes socially conventional. Nothing more, nothing less. Just imagine an atheist. And all of a sudden something happens to him in life that brings him close to God. And every time he takes a walk feeling the wind on his forehead and discovering life in front of him, he thanks God for being able to be part of this. Is this attitude before God not the correct one, - I mean, the attitude pursuant to God, the attitude that is exercised only as a form or as a rite? «

» A secret pre-romanticist «, Mill said.

» But it would not have been possible to talk to God via convention, the stonework of the church and the heart's purity, if everyone had been always free acting at random and these social conventions had never existed. These are the substance of tradition and compose the moments of our self-conception. It is only natural that they also display maxims of values «, Arthur explained.

» Yes, you are right! , I said, I just wanted to make it clear that today's moral decay about which we are talking over and over again, is also a victory for freedom in our history's development and that activities and intentions are very precious. «
» Reverend, what would God say to that? «, Miguel asked.

» God? «, Mill asked back looking a little surprised, » Do you believe God would take a stand? «

» Who else if not him. Who should be able to define justice if not God? «, Miguel replied.

Mill smiled, » Wait Miguel, I think that God doesn't stand outside of this world, looking at his creation crossing his arms up there in heaven thinking about what kind of complete idiots he created with only a few exceptions. I more believe that God and the creation are identical, in any which way. It's his creation and at the same time he reflects himself in his creation. You see a flower and you thank God for its existence. When you then touch and caress the flower what do you intentionally? Do you intend to really caress the flower? Or is it not because you pay your tender respects to the entire correlation of the created flower, your seeing eye and the Creator? God is in everything. And if there was a time where they tortured people in the name of God, then it represented a brick of experience of Creation. If people now are atheists and deny God, then this is also part of Creation. Strangely enough, God is always present as in the air breathing it in not mattering if you want to do it or not. Added to that, every single person has the possibility to find and recognize God inside themselves. The atheist, as does even the evil man. «

» Reverend «, I countered, » So what you are saying is that even evil necessarily belongs to Creation and God? «

Arthur joined the discussion: » The fact that evil exists shows us the justification for our conventions. Humanity experiences insights and passes them on as a convention and as a rule. Freedom of humanity is only a value, a power. But all activities have to follow regulations in order to believe and trust the other side. Leap of faith which we always desire and expect from each other, has to be guaranteed via a general language and social commitments. «
» Well ok «, Miguel added, » if evil belongs to Creation, so then to keep evil from developing further, Creation and God gave us regulations.

Then social regulations are wanted by God in order to lead Creation to a positive destination. But what bothers me with this idea is the fact that not all regulations are really good. Just think about the ones in dictatorships. «

» I think that here at this point a distinction is necessary «, Mill continued to explain, » a distinction between regulations that manifest at a particular time and form trends and fashion, and the ones that exist in a timeless way and above all appearances of time. «

» You know that I see the world from a conservative angle «, Arthur started, » and for me, values that are represented by the British monarchy and also the Vatican are values without which civilization could have never developed. You need living testimonials of values. «

» But, may I take the liberty of asking a skeptical question «, Miguel interposed, » the royal house as well as the Vatican play roles; they represent more of a figure, a form only and you ask yourself which kind of human being these figures are filled with. And I believe that this is the reason for the yellow press to give the masses a human angle to these celestial creatures by searching for human traits and publishing them under the name of scandal. «

» Yes «, Mill confirmed, » that's right, a scandal is a public offence and stands for the contradiction between all humanity and the dignified upper crust of heads of states as well as religious organizations. To some extent scandals can even be conciliatory for the heads´ roles.

Because this reveals that these people are also human. By this they primarily conserve their public image and their power. This sounds a little paradox, but this is the way it is. Scandal necessarily belongs to a monarchy, at least in a time of enlightenment. «

» Günther! You are our favorite German-British scandal. You are a living testimony for an existence of Prince Philip's life before he married Elizabeth II. He is by this a human being of flesh and blood, possesses a soul and is vulnerable like all of us «, Miguel quipped.

» There is also the question of how he sees himself «, Arthur threw into the round, » us four idiots sit together in this nice castle and are able to talk, believe, opine and speculate what we want, but our contact person is not sitting across from us. «

» I am real and may be able to cause effects «, I said.

» Bringing us back to the question «, so Miguel, » what reality is. Reality for our highly adored Prince Philip we are talking about is an image for the world and is mostly only described in the yellow press. It must be a lament for him to be an image for the world for his entire life. «

» Yes, a hard job indeed! «, Arthur added, » but you can assume that beyond this mask, behind this image the person is extremely vital and agile and recognizes what takes place around him. This person is not only an image. «

» One could think that the royal house is maybe interested in the publishing of one or the other picture by the media as they intend to avoid the public to see what really happens behind the scenes « ‚Miguel rumored, » there was not even an abstruse theory about the real reason for Lady Di´s death? «

» For God's sake «, Arthur exploded, » stop talking about this rubbish! The royal house is completely full of integrity and is upright against such allegations. Such images are only created by crazy men who aggrandize themselves comparable to the conspiracy theory of 9/11 in the United States. «

» You should not draw an image, it even says in the bible «, Mill said, » and means that we shouldn't draw a ready and complete image of the people as they all develop and the development should never stop. At least this applies to us as human beings. «

» But, what is if a person is only allowed to represent an image for others? «, Miguel asked.

» Well «, Arthur answered and looked at me seriously through his thick shell-rimmed glasses, » for Günther this means, in fact, that if Prince Philip himself would like to see you and speak to you, it wouldn't be possible as etiquette forbids him to. That is the way it is. «

» But «, I interfered, » I have communicated with the royal house. Partly via myself partly via a friend who is a lawyer. And I felt being close to it. Even when I call they immediately put me through to the relevant private secretaries. «

» And still «, Mill said now, » dear Günther, you have been told very clearly and explicitly that you should not continue to make your story public. «

» Indirectly they accept you, beloved Günther Focke «, so Miguel, » because they could have just ignored you, too. Please tell us what developed out of the exchange of letters with Buckingham Palace. Was there any progress? Were there any approaches? «

» Yes, you could say that contact became a little closer «, I said, » My lawyer tried to prove paternity via a genetic test. I wasn't very happy afterwards about this diplomatically doubtful suggestion, although I recognized that only such a test could give me certainty. «

» Is it in any way relevant with regards to the succession to the throne if you, Günther, really are the son of Prince Philip? «, Miguel was curious to know.

» Nonsense, not at all «, Mill explained, » only direct descendents of the queen have a right to the throne. «

» No Mill, I will have to remain poor for the rest of my life «, I said.

» And if it was possible to undertake such a genetic test? «, Miguel asked, » Are you entitled to conduct such a test in England at all? «

» Theoretically yes «, Arthur pointed out, » given the situation that Günther would have enough small change left over to afford a Barrister. Affiliation cases or other ones at which a blood examination would be quarreled over in court for a confirmation of paternity, these cases go to the » Crown Court «. The judge of such a Crown Court is only allowed to talk to a » Barrister «. Barristers are a sort of jurists, especially for this Crown Court. The procedure is described as follows: The client goes to the lawyer and he then contacts a Barrister. Lawyer and Barrister have a mutual rapport. The Barrister is paid by the lawyer of the client. The lawyer then has to be paid adequately by the client. The judge adjudicates not following any book of law, but according to the proportion of his rational arguments. «

» Is there no general book of law in England? «, Miguel asked.

» No, here in this case it is something different «, Arthur explained, » there are no laws in the English legislation under which you could subsume the verdict, but only volumes of precedences. Their essence might be used as a template for evaluating each case and its judgment. In our sample case, however, the argumentation for the demands of a genetic test decides. This means, Günther has to prove that his argumentation is rational. «

» To prove this, is what he is able to! «, so Mill.

Arthur continued: If he should be rejected by the Crown Court he can go to the Court of Appeal with his lawyer and Barrister in order to appeal the first verdict. If this fails the only last and highest level of jurisdiction would then be the House of Lords.
After this it's over. Normally such paternity cases are made public with the help of the press and then the candidates negotiate the case amongst each other. The cost for a regular Crown Court mounts up to £0.5m whereupon the largest part is the remuneration of the Barrister. «

» Why don't you simply take care of it for Günther? Or ask someone of your circles? «, Mill asked.

Arthur looked at Mill in a very severe way, » just because of that reason, my friend! «

» So, Günther is right when he says that his going public is in fact already part of his investigation into his own case? «, Miguel now asked.

» Well, I wouldn't see his case as self-evident as others especially because Prince Philip is a very influential person and is also restricted by his public image. «, Arthur explained.

» Sir Arthur! « A voice sounded through the room from behind us. It was Marian.

» Sir Arthur, a certain Fiona King registered at the gate. She said she talked to you and announced her visit. «, Marian reported.

» Oh, that's right! I almost forgot about her! Please let the young lady come in! «, so Arthur.

He stood up right away and went over to the chimney, added some pieces of log, filled up the glasses with Sherry and stood at the chimney focusing his view on the large folding door, just like a witness to a marriage.

He cleared his throat a few times. I noticed how agitated I was inside of me, almost nervous, it mumbled in my stomach. My god why did this girl come to this place at this exact moment, I thought. Miguel stood up and joined Arthur. Only Mill sat on his chair.

Steps were heard and then both sides of the folding door opened.

» Dear Fiona King! «, Arthur said and walked towards her. His voice sounded. She was wearing a slightly short off-white woolen skirt, black tights underneath it, a black sweater and a red leather jacket with a "Mille Miglia" sign. Her long black hair was plaited to an immense pigtail sliding around her neck and shoulders like a boa. I placed myself right next to Miguel. Mill now stood up.

» I am very grateful, Sir Arthur, for your hospitality, please excuse that I assail you, but the hotel I had booked has closed due to weather damage and I didn't know where else I could go in this weather! «, she said and you could tell how she was shivering.

» Günther! «, she shouted to me and embraced me immediately kissing me on the cheek, » my beloved, brave and crazy Günther! How nice to see you here! «
She turned to Miguel, he slightly clapped together the heels of his boots and bowed low, » Madame,

even emeralds would melt in front of your eyes! May I introduce myself; my name is Don Miguel Xavier, a Spaniard and crazy, too! «

Mill only took a little bow and said: Welcome at our moonstruck asylum! You are sent by heaven, so truthful, I will thank god for enriching our small patriarchal round with your juvenile and charming presence. «
Arthur handed to all of us a glass of sherry, » Welcome to our castle! « We finished the glasses sat down in our chairs and Fiona took a seat in between me and Miguel.

» I met with my new gallery owner and wanted to visit my friend Gina tomorrow afternoon. And I wanted to stay at that hotel over night, but they called me saying that they had weather damage at the hotel and because of that could not offer me a room. Then I remembered, Günther, that you once put a note with some phone numbers into my bag, back then, when I had visited you. And… «, she paused briefly and I saw how carefully Arthur was listening, » and I, I thought about just giving you a call, but didn't know that Sir Arthur White would answer on the other side of the phone. On this note only phone numbers with the corresponding addresses were listed, but no names «, she explained apologetically.

You could tell that she was a little bit ashamed. Arthur and Miguel observed her very precisely, although for different reasons.

» Fiona, may I call you Fiona? « Arthur asked, and she nodded her head, » please excuse me if I appear too obtrusive, but may I take a look at this note. I would like to check the numbers that are listed. «

Fiona reached in her brown handbag digging into it a little and handed him a business card. She looked at me in an interrogatory way; I shrugged my shoulders and said to her: » Wait Fiona, just wait! «

Arthur took his wallet out of his jacket, also taking out a business card. He compared both cards. He shook his head, stood up and went over to the chimney, filled up his glass with another Sherry, downing it in one shot he stooped to the chimney re-sorting the logs inside the fireplace. It was silent. We all looked at him waiting for him to say something.
Arthur cleared his throat, went over to his chair, lit a cigar and said: » Fiona, did Günther hand you this card? I mean, did you see him giving it to you? «, he asked clearing his throat again.

» Hm? No, not really, but why do you ask? I found this card in my handbag, days after having visited Günther and I assumed that he secretly put it in my handbag. Just like he, back then, had always put little packs of Davidoff or chocolate into my handbag or had sent it to me in a letter «, she explained, » so, really harmless and normal. Günther is like that. Once, he even put a strange watch in my pocket. «

Mill laughed and smiled. But I didn't really feel like laughing. Arthur looked very serious, took off his glasses and asked, » Fiona would it be possible that someone else put this card into your handbag without you noticing it? «

Fiona looked at me, » Günther what is going on here? «

» Fiona «, I said, » this is what we also would like to know, because it wasn't me putting this card in your handbag, for sure, and you know this card contains secret numbers known only to us four here and a few others. So the question arises now, who and why did someone put this card into your handbag. «

» Oh, my god, Günther, please tell me that this is not true. Have I been observed? Or did someone break into my house? Oh my god! Günther! «, she said and grabbed my hand. Fiona was cold. With my hands I tried to warm hers.

» Madame, you are safe here, isn't she, Arthur? Mill, say something! «, Miguel demanded.

» Fiona, don't worry, of course you are safe here with us, but also outside our vicinity. I have the feeling that this card story is more a hint to me by someone who wanted to tell me that I maybe should not have given these cards with the secret numbers to our friend Günther. I know that this statement raises lots of questions …«, Arthur cleared his throat once again, » You three know that we always meet at different places and that these places are extremely noble and, of course, I am not the owner of these castles or country estates, but … , « he shortly stopped, » I have my relations in society and me and also some others have the possibility that we can meet in these castles for a short time after agreeing on it. «

» But what does this have to do with Günther? «, Miguel asked.

» I think that there are people in this society who don't like to see Günther participating in these intimate rounds; to be more precise, I know definitely that they don't accept it, because it implies that I would help Günther with his intentions to make his case public «, Arthur explained.

» Oh, there is the case «, so Mill, » I have been waiting for the entire time, and just because Günther is present. That is what I said, wherever he is, we have a case. Marvelous, Günther, your entire life is a detective story. «

» Hopefully not at the end of his life, too! «, Arthur was joking.

» What do you mean by this, Arthur? «, Miguel asked.

» A joke, only a joke, really! «, Arthur revealed.

» Sir Arthur «, Fiona started to speak, being stopped immediately by him: » Please call me Arthur, I am old enough, we all call each other by our first names, and you now are part of our round, too! «

» Well Arthur «, she started again, » I don't really feel good about the fact that someone observed me and that someone put a business card with the numbers into my handbag at some point. I don't feel safe. «

» Yes «, Arthur added, » but you know, sometimes I would actually hope that somebody does observe me and thus gets the impression and conviction, even recording it on tape, with which accuracy and fidelity I and my closest confidants contrive to treat certain things. Sometimes it is better to be transparent instead of somebody getting an image of your person, but this image then displays only a misunderstanding. And as much as I have to condemn the fact that Günther can't be argued out of writing a book about his life and make it public, I have to respect his sense for the truth.

You can talk to him about everything and have the most trustful friend next to you. «

» We should have a toast to that «, Mill said, » Him up there always listens in anyway when people are making their confession! Miguel, would you please fill up our glasses? «

» Si, muy bien! «, Miguel said, filling up our Sherry glasses and handing them to us. » Please tell us, my beloved Fiona, how did you meet our friend Günther? «, Miguel wanted to know.

» Oh! «, she started to laugh, » Oh! Oh! That was really funny! «, Fiona laughed very loud, covering her mouth with her hand; she started to grunt, then to even snigger, bending over her upper body and starting to laugh aloud. It nearly sounded like a bawling. The entire round, being engaged and anxious about bitter thoughts before, now had to go along this laughing with only Arthur abstaining.

» Well, oh, Günther, yes dear gentlemen, this was very amusing «, and she wiped her tears from her face, » well, it was like this «, and she broke out laughing again like a madwoman, this time joined by the entire round, Arthur included.

She deeply breathed out, » A moment please, dear gentlemen, just a moment «, she tried to gather herself holding her nose with her hand, breathing in profoundly.

» Well, it was in autumn of last year, I was at home in my little castle and the atmosphere in my family was rather depressing. Margret, the little daughter of my sister Sarah was suffering badly from kidney cancer. Sarah was with her at the intensive care unit at hospital and prayed that our little one would survive this cancer. And I was at home by myself and totally frustrated, because I had desperately tried to collect 50,000 pounds for a kidney transplant. I was so desperate that I even tried to extort money from someone whose name I don't want to mention here now. I was totally desperate waiting for the hospital to call. Outside, the wind trumpeted around the house, it was freezing and I thought everything will soon collapse, the world, the house, life, just everything. All of a sudden somebody rang at the door. I opened and there was Günther, dressed with an anorak and with a small hairless dog in his arms. He looked at me and started to stumble, » well, my, my name is Focke, Günther Focke, I am private detective «, and right in this moment the small dog started to pee on Günther´s sleeve and a stream gushed in front of my door, directly in front of my feet and Günther stood there like a tin soldier not knowing what to do while a stream was dripping right on his shoes. «

Everybody in the round smiled.

» Well, and then «, she reported, » I took this tiny little hairless dog out of his hands, wrapped him in a bath robe and sat him down, no, it was a female dog, exactly, Rachel was her name, and sat her down to let her dry in front of the fireplace. And this is how I met Günther. He helped me through this horrible day in a very lovely way. On the next day then Margret passed away. Günther brought me to the hospital and we picked up Sarah who was devastated. He then drove back to Corby. At that point I didn't know that he allegedly is the illegitimate son of Prince Philip. He didn't say a word about it. A month later, when I had an appointment in London, I visited him in Corby. He just got back from somewhere cutting fir trees or something like that, he looked all disheveled and I was in his garage where I saw these three pictures on the wall, pictures of Prince Philip, Prince Charles and him, Günther Focke. «

» Lovely «, Mill said, » we all would have liked to be there with you! «

» So, Rachel is a female dog? And doesn't have any hair either? «, Miguel asked dumbfounded.

» Yes, once we met with an Arabic diplomat and wanted to discuss world politics. It's been a while. I had organized a huge Bedouin tend, equipped with a water pipe and a dozen pillows, carpets and plush in order to let our Arabic friend feel as comfortable as possible. This was at England's East coast. I have a friend there who owns some land there at the coast. As we were sitting there enjoying our discussion, all of a sudden this little hairless dog came inside this tent, sniffing at everything and from that moment on hasn't left Günther.

» What should I do? «, I asked, » Chase her away? The weather was already warm, but the dog was freezing. I took her with me and tried all my best to stimulate the growth of hair, but nobody was able to figure out why this dog lost her hair. «

» There is this theory «, Mill pointed out, » according to which there is a natural affinity in between dogs and their owners. I recently heard, for example, about a blind person who has already gone through four guide dogs. «

» How is that, Reverend? «, Miguel asked him, » what did she do to the poor dogs?

» All dogs became blind, too, in time. Nobody knows why. Of course, unpleasant situations occurred by this. Just imagine you are blind, you stand at a street corner and your guide dog doesn't see anything either! «, Mill answered.

» But I still have all my hair, Reverend «, I brought up.

» My dear Günther, but your skin is harmed. «, Fiona mentioned, » but tell me, how is little Rachel doing now? «

» Oh, in the meantime some hair grew again «, I reported, » Marie, a fashion designer, has knitted some capes, sweaters, caps, partly also made out of leather, so she doesn't freeze so much. «

» Fiona, you said you extorted money from somebody? Did Günther come to you because of this? «, asked Miguel.

» Yes, he had found me via a letter of mine addressed to my sister which he … found on her at the university. But I confessed it to him right away. I was so desperate and Günther understood … «

» That «, Arthur interrupted, » Sir Arthur can be a bad man and that Sarah was expecting a baby from him and I, the happily married Arthur, would not take care of the child, and in this desperate situation was justifiably blackmailed by Fiona. «

» You? You, Arthur? You of all people? «, Mill shouted in an appalled way.

» Senor! «, – Miguel commented.

» Yes Mill, I confess it. I have to confess it. It is about time. It cannot be that Günther and Fiona know about something in this circle that you two don't. It's ridiculous. Well, I met Sarah when I was studying law. And she was extraordinarily talented, studious and very beautiful. I had something going on with her and yes: she got pregnant. Then I suddenly received a blackmail letter which said Sarah had been kidnapped and I should pay £50,000. Of course, no police should be alarmed. So I called Günther and he came over right away. I told him what I knew and he started to investigate this case. Shortly afterwards he came back and he said he had solved the case «.

Arthur cleared his throat, went over to the fireplace and put some more wood on.

» And what has happened to the child? «, Mill was curious to know, » Do you at least look after it in a proper way? «

» Oh, I sent Sarah £100,000! «, he answered.

» Sir Arthur, Arthur «, Fiona said carefully.

» I know, Fiona, the story turned into a tragedy. In fact «, he said turning to me, » I wanted to find out via another detective how Sarah was doing and he reported to me that she had lost her child a few days after I had delivered the money via a messenger. The detective told me, furthermore, that Sarah already had a little daughter who had passed away due to kidney failure. It became clear to me that Fiona had intended to use the money for a kidney transplant. But it was too late. Back then I didn't know about little Margret. Nobody told me about her. «

» In other words «, so Mill, » you paid double compensation for Sarah, whereupon half would have been enough to rescue Sarah's little child Margret? «

» Yes, Mill, I know, it's sheer lunacy «, so Arthur.

» Phew! «, Miguel commented, » what a tragedy! Why didn't you, Fiona, contact Arthur right away or why didn't your sister do it. Arthur would have given you the money for sure. «

» Miguel, what do you think how many times Sarah and I talked about it. But Sarah was too scared to tell Arthur that she already had a child.

I think her respect towards Arthur as a man of his stature and as a lecturer was enormous. And maybe she also felt guilty that she got pregnant by him. «
» How is Sarah doing now, is she mad at me? «, Arthur asked like a little boy.

» I think she is rather mad at herself. She knows that the loss of Margret and her unborn child had not necessarily had to happen, if she had been honest and direct from the beginning and had talked openly to you, Sir. «

» You know, Arthur, « Mill started, » that people hold you in high esteem? Virtually dread! This is also because of the fact that you can sometimes react very heavily and bring down people just with your arguments. This is not good, Arthur, but I already talked to you about this. Here and there you could act a little more conciliatory. You always think if you donated 100,000 pounds to a foundation you would provide your share to the world in a sufficient way. But you only do this in order to enjoy yourself in your own sunlight. You then are invited somewhere and are entitled to hold one of your brilliant speeches, but you don't see the real misery in your nearest surroundings. You, the benefactor! And then you wonder why others fear you and they don't open up to you in their bleak misery which you could easily alleviate. «

» I know Mill, I know «, Arthur stood up and walked slowly to the folding door. He opened it and closed it again behind him.

Silence fell over the circle of friends.

Miguel tried to break the ice by asking: » Günther! What about another one of your detective stories? Maybe one that will lift our spirits? «

» Oh, Miguel, life and the detective stories all have their little and big tragedies. When you need a detective, something somewhere has already got out of hand. «

» You said, - and you see, I listen to you carefully - that you had been arrested by the police because you were suspected for smuggling? «, Miguel remembered, » please tell us how that occurred. «

» A dumb story, really «, I said, » although everything had started so harmlessly. Actually, I should have investigated in this case, but the police were entirely involved in it and I needed a little break. Back then I was with my friend Ralph on my courtyard, on which I had parked a VW Passat from Germany. «

» Hehe «, Fiona laughed, it's wonderful that Günther has such a weakness for these German estate cars. Have you been to his house? He had three cars parked there. And in one of those he wanted to put a three cylinder engine! Sorry, Günther, I won't interrupt you again! «
» What kind of car do you drive? « Miguel asked.

» An old black MGB, but during winter time a green Peugeot 206, and you, Sir? «, she asked back.

» A Mercedes SL 55, it is also black, but it is an older model. The new ones have such lovely characteristics, which reflect every detail of the car. «

» Oh, Senor understands about art! «, - Fiona remarked.

» No, only of beauty and truth, Madame! «, Miguel blinked at her noticing at the same time that I was following their discussion and backed out of it physically.

I continued: » I actually wanted to demonstrate to Ralph how to take off the back door of this Passat estate car. Fiona is right; I am quite fond of VW Passats. Recently, someone hit the back of my red Passat. What a pity, it's completely destroyed. Anyway, Ralph and I were on my business yard. As I found out later my business yard had been under surveillance by the customs authority. Murdy, too, was with us. He told us that he was waiting for a container transport which had arrived from China and which he had to unload.

I asked Murdy about what was loaded in this container. » Well, shoes from China «, he answered like a duck takes to water, in a way as if it was naturally for an Englishman to stand on a yard waiting for a container with shoes from China. It actually should have been suspicious to me, but I didn't care.

Ralph and I left the courtyard with the backdoor of the Passat. I drove to Ralph's house, we unloaded the door and I planned on taking off to London. As I was passing by the yard again I, in fact, saw this container standing there. I stopped in front of the container and noticed that it was loaded with boxes. I got out of my car and asked Murdy if he needed help with unloading it. » No, thanks, I'll handle it «, he said callously. At the container I saw a half open box with a pair of plastic shoes sticking out. Well then, I thought, if he felt like unloading the container until the day after tomorrow without any help, I would have better things to do.

So as I was going back to my car all of a sudden somebody attacked me. I automatically tried to defend myself and – however – my foot hit his neck. Then also a woman lunged out and shouted: » Customs & Excise! «

She fluttered with her ID in front of me. How nice, I thought. The other one rattled a little and the woman told me that I was arrested.

» Arrested? «, I asked astonished. I didn't want to explain the story of my life now, but at home I am a normal civilian who doesn't need to anticipate that he is being observed.

Then another person came over to us. It was the officer on duty. I was quite annoyed, so I looked around to see if there were maybe more officers behind the fence lunging at me all of a sudden. No, not again. The officer told me that I was under arrest and asked whether I would go with them voluntarily or in handcuffs. Of course, I followed them voluntarily.

I tried to explain to him that I didn't know that this officer - who was still gasping for air - was actually an officer. A police car drove up and I had to get in it. It is now also common in England that an officer holds your head when entering a police car so you don't bump your head. They learned that from the Americans, like so many other things, you understand? «

» Like in a movie «, Miguel inserted, » they should try this with me. I think in Spain the Guardia Civil would not touch your head. «

» Right at that moment I realized that my arrest and the police surveillance could have something to do with the container. I asked the officer if my assumption was true.

»Yes! «, he answered, » in fact! You seem to know the case well, as we assumed! «

» Oh «, I said, » You have really arrested the wrong person. «

He replied to me: » We will clear this up at the police station. «

When the car took off I saw that also Murdy was arrested and brought away in another police car.

At the police station I was handed over to the arresting officer, who informed me that I was being retained for suspicion of smuggling cigarettes to the value of £1.0m. I was astonished. Indeed I smoke a lot, but such a large amount was even too much for me. They then put me in a prison cell and I had to wait to be interrogated.

The prison cell was dirty; the walls seemed to be covered with faeces. I felt claustrophobic in there, hyperventilating and getting heart rhythm disturbances. «

» This is horrible, Günther, what they did to you! «, Fiona said and reached for my right hand.

» Well, Fiona, wait, the story is not over yet. I called for the officer and explained to him that I had to leave this cell urgently or he would need to call a doctor. The officer took me out of there and brought me to the exercise yard. There now I had to wait for my interrogation. They took everything away from me. My house keys, of course, too. As I found out later, police officers invaded my house and searched everything for smuggled goods. «

» How is it possible to find something in your house? «, Fiona laughed.

» Exactly, a thought with a humorous touch, as the garage of my yard partly extents into several levels of my house and it is quite difficult without my inner plan to find things.

Then, finally, I was brought to the interrogation room. There was a woman sitting and a man from the customs investigations department. I was asked if I needed a lawyer. I declined as I had nothing to hide.

» Please turn on the tape recorder. Before that I don't even think about saying a word! «, I insisted. They had the right to detain me not because they had evidence against me for alleged smuggling, but because I had injured a police officer when he jumped on me.

The tape recorder was turned on. The officers introduced themselves as: » Her Majesty's customs and excise Officers. «

» Gentleman «, I admonished, » if you act in Her Majesty's service, then please behave like it! «

» Somehow this sentence had its impacts «, I continued as the female officer introduced herself without the part "in Her Majesty's service" and wanted to know from me what I knew about these smuggled goods.
» I don't know anything about it, the only thing I know is that, well, there were shoes from China in this container, weren't there? Murdy told me this, when I asked him if he needed help unloading the container. «
Furthermore, the officers asked me about what kind of relation I had to this person and they showed me a picture with my friend Ralph, me and Murdy on it.

» What a nice color photo «, I said, » when did you take it? Listen, this person « – and I pointed on Ralph – » is my friend and I would always trust him. The other one's name is, as far as I know, Murdy. I don't know him very well. I share rent of this business yard with Steward, a friend of mine. «

The officers kept on asking me questions. » Where is this Steward? «

» I don't think he is in England at the moment «, I countered. » Two days ago I talked to him on the phone and he mentioned that he was abroad for business. «

Apparently this response was enough for them because at this point they told me that in the meantime they had searched my house and that they took my phonebook and other documents for investigation purposes. I protested immensely, because my phonebook contained all the important phone numbers of my detective work and, of course, also the numbers of Buckingham Palace and Princess Sophia, the sister of Prince Philip who lived in Germany, and, to tell you the truth, I didn't want to leave those to some eager customs officers. And on top of that, in connection with this alleged cigarette smuggling situation, for God's sake. I thought, maybe they call the Palace later. They promised me to just make a copy of the numbers sending all original items back to me afterwards. That's in fact what they did - by personal messenger. «

Meanwhile Arthur came back in and said: » Don't care a fig for it, Günther; three decades ago I was in prison in Stockholm. A funny story, too. But it is not that important. «
» Unbelievable what we get to know this evening! «, Mill pointed out.

» May I sit down at the fireplace? I'm still cold! «, Fiona asked.

» Please do«, Arthur said, » feel like home! «

Miguel's glance followed Fiona, nudging Arthur and I heard him whispering to him, » Look Arthur, how small her bottom is, she hardly has breasts either, she is lithe and lissome just like a mythical creature, like an elf, she must be a higher creature, believe me! «

If Miguel only knew how right he was with his quick fire observation. In fact, Fiona was a rare mixture of sensibility, intelligence and reality and she had a real sympathetic outlook on people as I have never come across before in a woman. She didn't even care that I sometimes looked at her as if she were an icon. She looked at my bashful attitude towards her with a light sense of humor and she would make me feel good inside without ever causing too much excitement. She was human and, in an intelligent way, she didn't take advantage of it at all. «

Arthur hardly took notice of Miguel's comment. He seemed to be very involved in his thoughts. Mill had listened, chuckled to himself and shook his head saying to Arthur, » what, my dear, did you do when you were gone? «

» I made some phone calls and went over to Marian. Somebody is visiting her, too. An artist couple passing through «, he explained. » I had to gather myself a little, you know. I am not as cold and arrogant as you always say. «

» Dear Arthur, we have known each other for such a long time now, you are like a mad man flitting between being sociable like Sir Arthur and being part of the soul of the sentimental Arthur without even noticing it! Why can't you be Arthur more often! «, Mill said and suggested, » how about indulging in a bottle of champagne now at this time of telling the truth? «

» Splendid idea! «, Miguel replied, » I am craving something sparkling, Senor Focke, may I offer you a Monte Christo? «

» Oh, I would like to have one, too «, Fiona noted.

Arthur replied, » Dear friends I have here some exquisite Dareer and Cleef, please, help yourself. I will go and pick up the champagne. «

Mill nodded his head, and as soon as Arthur disappeared through the folding door he said: » It's new to me, too, that Arthur walks by himself, although his leg seems to have got worse. You know that our discussions clear the air! I think it's good that so many things came up today «.

» It made me jump when I called here and all of a sudden I had my blackmail victim on the phone. I almost hung up «, Fiona mentioned, » but, I thought, if Arthur is a friend of Günther then it can't be so terrible. I needed some courage to come here. «

» If you, dear Fiona, had not come «, Mill replied, » Arthur would have never brought himself to confess that he had a son with your sister. I saw Arthur being so introverted. Almost remorseful. A rarity. «

» I feel very comfortable in this circle of gentlemen, thank you «, Fiona said changing the subject. It was her style to avoid going into things into depth; not because of ignorance, but rather to make the truth be pure. When you talked to her about it she used to smile gently saying, » I am just gracious «.

The folding door shook and Arthur came back in with a bottle of champagne. » I couldn't find a bucket «, he shouted.

» Well, I think it will do as it is «, and Fiona smiled. While Arthur poured the champagne Fiona looked at me saying, » Günther, I thought that you only drink Alster beer? «
I smiled back, » Champagne is an exception! «

» Miguel «, Arthur started, » You said some time ago that you wanted to go to Brazil this year. What takes you there? Pleasure or business? «

» Most certainly both «, Mill said.

» Recently I met a very interesting young man who told me he had the intention to establish a worldwide diamond and gold exchange based in Berlin. He had very interesting contacts in Bangkok even in Rwanda. He invited me to join him. But it is a very dangerous thing above all in Brazil and Rwanda. Such a business needs to be established carefully and at the same time has to be diplomatically secured «, Miguel reported.

» I can already sense a new case for Günther «, so Mill.

» Well I don't hope so, but I once actually had some work to do in Brazil «, I replied.

» Anything to do with diamonds and gold? «, Miguel wanted to know.

Fiona clapped her hands, » Günther, please, tell us! «

» Yes, Günther «, so Miguel, » please give us an insight into life in Brazil and into the criminal world! «, Miguel replied.

So I started:

» It was at the end of April and it was already getting warm. I kept myself busy with paperwork which I normally never have time for. The phone rang.
» Hello, Mr. Focke, this is Fritz Hinnerk speaking! «, the voice said.

He was the son of a lawyer from Hamburg. I knew him from my time as a soldier for the German military, the Bundeswehr. His father was also known to me from my time back then with Wolfgang Xanke.

» Günther, my father died «, he let me know right away.

» Oh my god, I am so sorry, Fritz, what can I do for you? «, I tried to help. » I opened the will at our lawyer's office. And it says that the inheritance should be divided between me and my father's brother, uncle Rudi. But the problem now is nobody knows where uncle Rudi is. A long time ago - I was still a little child - he allegedly went to Brazil on a cargo ship and he never came back «, Fritz Hinnerk reported.

Are there any letters or addresses in an address book or are there common friends, school friends, girl friends, of weddings, of funerals, or maybe any business contacts? «, I asked him.

» In my father's address book he has only listed clients from Hamburg and we don't need to call those. I couldn't find any other address books. The only things I found are these postcards from Brazil. And only signed with "Rudi", but with no reply address on them! «, he explained.
» How many postcards did you find? «, I asked him.

» About four or five «.

I told him to send me these cards to England. I then would contact him, of course.

» Well, Fritz «, I added, » given the fact that you are in Hamburg why don't you go to the marine authority and ask for the cargo ship crew list where Rudolph Hinnerk was registered on a trip to Brazil. «

Fritz asked as if not quite sure: » Yes, and I can get a list there just like that? «

I then explained: » Members of a crew who don't come back from going on shore have to be registered and notify the authorities. If you ask for the name they will provide you with this information. «

Fritz said good-bye and we arranged to talk in a few days.

Some days later I received mail from Fritz Hinnerk. I opened the envelope and meticulously analyzed the postcards. On the front there were typical motifs of sunsets.

Using a magnifying glass, I inspected the seal on the postage stamp. Fritz wrote in the enclosed letter that Rudolph Hinnerk was registered at the marine authority in 1962 by David Schuh, the captain of the "Rote Lore", a cargo ship which was loaded with iron ore.

Good, I thought, so where exactly did cargo ships head for back then. So I had to search for ports which were used as trans-shipment centers for iron ore in Brazil. At first I looked at a large map of Brazil. The places which I was able to identify on the stamps were all near the port of Macau. In addition I researched that Macau was a huge stopping over centre for iron ore.

I booked my flight via several airports from London to Rio de Janeiro. I generally try to take as many short flights as possible. You don't actually save time this way, especially not if you want to get from England to Brazil, but the distance between departures and arrivals is still shorter.

From Rio I then flew to Recife with a Cessna. Recife is the only airport in the area there. Then I took a taxi and was driven to a village called Macauzinho. I must admit that the journey was extremely uncomfortable.

Sometimes we had to even get out to clear the road of obstacles and at times the road seemed to be more like a path. My driver assured me he was a dedicated rally driver. And probably also a good solo entertainer as he turned his head back to me in a discussion while driving or showed me regional distinctions; he must have known every bend on the road by heart. Nevertheless we arrived in Macauzinho safely, a provincial town in Brazil. The coast of the South Atlantic was about 30 miles away. First of all I tried to find a hotel. The lady at the reception spoke English and a little German. Her name was Helena and she was stunningly beautiful.

I ordered some food, a Mao de Vaca, and went to bed shortly afterwards. I was exhausted. My habit of always flying short distances was quite a stressful experience over this long distance between England and Brazil, because you have to exit one plane, wait for the next one, check in, and so on. My journey there lasted two days. After flying from Toronto to Washington and later having the chance to walk around for an hour in Kansas, I sat next to a nice lady on the flight from San Francisco to Miami. She was a manager of a pretty big company and often traveled to Europe. She promised to give me a call next time she was near London.

On the next day I took a taxi and was driven to Macao.

I walked through the city and looked at the port where Rudolph Hinnerk had arrived with the Rote Lore and supposedly had decided to stay here forever, that is if he really did stay here for decades in the end.

What could have been his motive to disembark and to build a new life here in Macau? Did he have any contacts here? Did he just want to drop out as others did back in those days who were tired of society and all political tensions? Did he find a woman here? Did he have children? What could have ensured his survival here since the beginning of the sixties since when he had never come back to Germany? Or did he maybe go from Macau to the nearby Recife, where the possibilities of employment were much greater in a city full of cultural venues, businesses and with over one million inhabitants than was the case in poor Macau with its iron-ore drop off point. Olinda was also a possible spot in so far as that Olinda was more attractive to people from Northern Europe thanks to its climate. I read about Olinda that an odd and colorful tribe of poets, musicians, fun-loving contemporaries, in short: a lot of crazy people gathered there. Did Rudolph Hinnerk belong to them at some point? I would never have the chance to find him in such a melting pot.

Macau itself lies on the river „Rio Das Prinhas". All the cargo ships arrived through this river mouth. I admired the captains how they managed to navigate their ships through the narrow mouth to the port. Every time such a cargo ship arrived, the old and ravaged dockland came to life.

From every corner hundreds of people gathered helping to ship the ore from the cargo trains. Sailors crossed the squares; beautiful girls strolled along the quay.

I tried to think about how I could find Rudolph Hinnerk. The investigation was not easy, because I don't speak any Portuguese and the people there didn't understand English. I took a taxi back to Macauzinho. Helena was at my hotel and I explained to her that I would need an interpreter. Helena told me that I had to ask the manager for that. The South American custom was to pay for that. Helena cost $ 50 per day! How can I declare that in my statement of expenses? It didn't matter.

Either way, she was my interpreter - and nothing else.

We took a taxi to Macau. Helena changed before we left. She was visibly enjoying the adventure trip with me. And this fact made me happy, too. Somehow I regretted to be here on business. I couldn't stop studying her on our journey and also smelling her perfume and body odor. Without a doubt, her family was from this region. She was completely of Afro-Brazilian origin. But she would not tell me where she had learned the few words of German she knew. She looked at me and asked what we were actually looking for. » I'll tell you about it tonight, Helena, when we have some time! «, I answered her. Helena remained silent and stared at me for a long period.

When we finally arrived in Macau I asked in some restaurants where I would be able to find people from Europe.

An older man told me that he once met one person who came from the United States. And this man had opened up a business in Macau. I asked him about what kind of shop this was. » Oh, a night club! «, the man said. My ears perked up. I asked him if he could remember his name. Unfortunately he couldn't.

» But wait, there is a bar where you could get some further information «, he said. I offered

Helena my arm and we went over to this bar. It was nearly 5:00 in the afternoon and sweltering. When we arrived Helena asked the bar tender for the manager. It almost appeared to me as if she could deal with any type of situation. But why not, she was a native to these regions.

In the meantime the bar tender told us that a European had opened up the "Farolito" night club years ago. We stayed there for a while looking for protection from the sun underneath the thatched roof of a veranda. Helena examined me for a long time. At about 8:00 in the evening we both went to take a look at this club. We sat down at the bar and asked the bar tender for the manager. He wasn't there. And it seemed like it was out of place to ask for the manager here. The barman's fierce Latino stare could have melted an iceberg. I cringed. Helena pulled at my shirt and said, » Come on Günther, let's get out of here as fast as possible! « I understood. We took a taxi and drove back to the hotel. When we arrived there I asked Helena if she had to take care of the hotel again or if she was free.

» Mister Focke «, she said, » you have already paid for the whole day! «

So we went over to the hotel bar and Helena ordered some Tiragostos for us.

She was curious to know what I was exactly looking for in this remote town. I told her very abstractly that I was here on behalf of somebody in order to find a person who came here from Germany a long time ago and who had inherited a fortune. She laughed and repeated » a fortune? « How is it, Guntero? Don't you know that people here would do anything for a fortune? Didn't you see all these tens of thousands of retirantes in Recife who vegetate all year long on the outskirts of town and suffer from all kinds of diseases, Malaria, Diphtheria and diarrhea? «

» I was in Recife only for a short period, Helena. I know that South America is very poor just like wherever else on this planet people are poor, desperate, hungry, sick, full of pain and humiliation. I know about it as I know the starry sky above me and still I cannot change anything. Sometimes I have difficulties to take care of myself and my next of kin. Be sure, Helena, distress, misery and desperation are not only a South American phenomenon. The world is still a labyrinth equipped with landmines and furnished with dungeons and grotesqueness making you dizzy and posing yourself the question why do I do all this and why do I still believe in something. «

The next day I bought a magazine, a weekly German magazine. I took off for Farolito again, but this time without Helena.

It was too dangerous to conduct my investigations in a night club with such a beautiful woman if it wasn't clear what was going on in this night club.

Equipped with this magazine I went to the Farolito bar, this time I did not go directly to the bar and sat down at a table in a distance. The bar lady came over and I ordered an Alster beer. Of course they didn't have Alster beer as I was in Brazil. So I ordered a beer and a lemonade and mixed it myself. While doing this I inevitably had to think about this famous colleague of mine who in contrast to me worked in Her Majesty's service and preferred his drink "shaken, not stirred".

» Günther «, Fiona laughed, » you are agent double-0 eight! «

» We have known this for a long time! «, Mill smiled.

» Yes «, Fiona said in an impertinent way, » Günther is the real undercover agent of the British crown, he is really working unofficially: Not in Her Majesty's service! «

» Does this Alster beer exist in Britain at all? «, Miguel asked.

» The name here for it is Shandy «, Mill explained.

I carried on: » Four nights I spent there in this club, always equipped with my magazine under my arm and with a stirred Alster. I thought this German would hopefully recognize the magazine and ask me out of curiosity if he could take a look at it. My magazine was the distinctive mark at a blind date like, for example, a rose in the buttonhole. And the blind date was with a German, to be more precise with Rudi Hinnerk.
And in fact, on the fourth night somebody came from behind and talked to me.

» May I take a look at your magazine? «, a man asked.

I turned around and said: » Yes, of course, but only if you are Rudi Hinnerk!

The man turned his head aside and said:

» I am sorry, but my name is Xiniero! But, mister, maybe I could be useful and help you. Excuse me, but what was your name? «

He was still a real gentleman of the old school, white suit, straw hat, and a grey-white beard. He sat down with me.

» My name is Focke, Günther Focke. I am a private detective! «, I introduced myself.

» Oh, Mister Focke, don't get me wrong, but I have been living here for a long time and have experienced a lot of amateurs dressed in the most harmless clothes and since the time when Miguel Arraes, Francisco Juliao and also Don Helder Camara were fugitives we are very skeptical, especially with regard to spies, agents or as we call them: private detectives! «

What an introduction, I thought, what kind of game is this?

» Excuse me, Mister «, I said, » but I really don't understand a word of what you are trying to tell me here. I don't know all these names and what you mean by amateurs. «

He looked at me in a nice way, folded his hands and quickly looked towards the bar. I followed his eyes and recognized the bar tender who had been so rude to me the first time I came here.

At this moment the bar tender nodded and within a second two gorillas in military dress with Che Guevara berets, plaited pigtails and sun glasses sat down with us. They smiled at me. One then said: » Should we show our friend here the Kalvary Mountain? «

I reached for my Alster beer and had a sip. Something went wrong. What did they mean with Kalvary Mountain? Nothing good, that's for sure?

» Listen dear gentlemen, « I wanted to grab my wallet out of the inner pocket of my jacket to show them my passport, » I prove you that I am an authorized private detective in Germany and Great Britain and I really don't understand ... « Where was my wallet?
They stood up, grabbed my arm and right at that moment I could hear a female voice speaking Portuguese. I couldn't understand what she said. The men let me go immediately, and Xiniero stood up and said in German, » Helena, you know this man? «

» Oy! He lives with us in the Georgea, he is a friend! «

I was still standing slightly hunched over with my arms bent and a little bemused and astonished by Helena, who apparently knew this Xiniero and by her saving me from the walk to the Kalvary mountain, whatever this was.

The two bodyguards bowed in front of Xiniero and left.

Helena came over to our table, sat down and said, » Rodolfo let him talk. He is no amateur if you thought that. I found his wallet with money and his documents in his room. He is apparently searching for somebody here who inherited a fortune in Germany. Helena handed him my wallet. I was astonished.

Then he got more down to the point » Why do you want to talk to Mister Hinnerk? « I explained to him that Bertram Hinnerk passed away and his son Fritz is now looking for his uncle and sent me to find him.

Xiniero obviously startled moved backwards with his chair and asked me: » Bert is dead? « Here was the proof. That Xiniero is Hinnerk.

» How old is Fritz now? «, he asked me now full of trust.

» Fritz is now 35 years old «, I reported.

» Oh my God, already a young man. It was so long ago. Oh my God! «, he talked more to himself than to me.

» Are you Rudolph Hinnerk? «, I asked him now more precisely.

» Yes, of course. They turned Hinnerk to Xiniero here in Brazil «, he explained to me and let me know of further examples of new names created by the Portuguese –Brazilian style.

» Please excuse my initial mistrust towards you. I have nothing to hide, but have to pay attention with regards to my club here! «, he added.

But I would need a proof for you being Rudolph Hinnerk. A passport, for example, would do the job «, I said to him.

» Yes, of course. Come over again tomorrow afternoon and I will have my passport on me «, he said clearly.

On the next day I took Helena with me and met Rudi 'Xiniero' again. He showed me a very faded document on which a stamp of Hamburg St. Pauli was still recognizable. It was only a shred, but an official and acceptable document.

He appeared somehow pensive and said: » You know, Mister Focke, you couldn't know that I am the real father of Fritz. Back then I separated from his mother and came to Brazil. You said that Fritz thinks I would be his uncle. Does this mean that Bert put him up? «

» Oh yes «. I said: » Bertram Hinnerk had officially adopted Fritz. And Fritz knows about it, but he doesn't know who his real father is. «

» And what about his mother «, Xiniero asked.

» I don't know. She had given him up for adoption «, I mentioned.

» Oh God, and now you are sent by him who doesn't even know what kind of uncaring father he has. I shouldered a heavy burden. Mister Focke, I don't think I should return to Germany. What should I say to Fritz? « He shook his head.

» You must bear in mind that in your brother's will it says that the inheritance should be divided between you and your son! This was the actual reason for me coming here! «, I said.

» An inheritance? You know I am so rich here and am already 70 years old. I don't need anything else «, he countered.

» In this case we need to go to a lawyer and you have to sign a release declaration. This I have to confirm in a statutory declaration in Germany and then everything will be ok. «

» Then let's do it this way! I know a good lawyer here. He speaks fluent English. «

After we cleared the formalities at the lawyer's office in Macauzinho we wished each other good luck and bid farewell. I was a little surprised by how tragic this case turned out. I hadn't reckoned on that.

The next day I ordered a taxi to Recife. I was standing in the hotel's entrance hall and Helena and I looked at each other. It was a little like being in a movie. Just this moment. This situation. This out of this world around us moment! The taxi sounded the horn. I picked up my luggage and left.

In Recife I had to wait almost an hour for my plane which was supposed to take me to Rio. I was standing in the sun wearing a hat. My mouth was all dry. The plane finally arrived. The next flight was a non-stop flight from Rio to Hamburg.

» I briefly thought about stopping by in Wremen. But I just wanted to send the signed documents to Fritz's lawyer and then fly back to England on the next plane. «

» Wow! «, Fiona expressed, » did you have something going on with this Helena? Come on! «

» No Fiona «, I countered, » I really didn't «.

» Isn't it noticeable «, Mill said, » that so many cases that you have investigated are to do with missing identities and also with illegitimate children. Didn't you often have to think bout your own case? «

» Yes, Mill «, I confirmed, » the investigations were always keeping an eye on who and where. The man lost in space. But of course there were other cases, just for example the bomb and the blackmail story or the case with the girl in the moors. «

» Günther! «, Arthur said, » if you, after all these cases, want to resume and give advice to people how to make their life happier and easier in such way that the private detective would only need to search for missing bicycles and not always for such real life tragedies, what would you say then? «

I looked at everybody in our circle. » Arthur «, I said, » maybe each life, each individual's understanding of the world is detective work and nothing else than a reconstruction. It took a long time for me to realize how important history is even for us. I cannot tell you what would be necessary so that a private detective would not have to deal with these real life tragedies, but only with simple problems and demands.

What a question, Arthur! What is certain is if history has caused feelings to be hurt and this history always reaches into the future, then the present will have to relieve the pain of hurt feelings for the future. There is nothing else to do than take care of our children, that they make it safely to

school, no accidents happen and that next time - whatever it might be - will be better. «
» But without any pain we often don't feel anything «, so Mill.

» Yes, we are happy if we create a life without any pain, but then we are not able to recognize anymore how our vulnerability makes us forget about our soul «, Arthur stated.

Miguel breaking the silence said, » Günther, today we have learnt really a lot. It wasn't my intention to come here in order to learn anything. Anyway, I don't think that anybody came here, said something or listened to the others in order to learn something. We weren't here to learn, to discover something or to take back with us anything substantial. But in the end it is like that. «
» Coincidences «, Arthur said, » these are also coincidences which meet like agents who agreed upon creating appearances, stories and insights. «
» A mighty sword that you cite, Sir Arthur«, Fiona underlined.

» What Günther «, Miguel asked, » will you do? Will you continue communicating with Buckingham Palace hoping to get an opportunity to be heard? «
» The very real story of Günther Focke will continue for sure, and, as I already mentioned, the making

public of my life regardless of from which point onwards it will start, will be able to explain and bear testimony to many lives, stories, the past and other moments which should be reported «, I pointed out.

» Absolutely «, Mill confirmed, » we already observed that your going public is part of your detective work and part of your own life. After all, through what you have told us we were able to notice for all intents and purposes that your allegations are justified. In court nothing else was ever requested when somebody wanted to make his own claim public. «

» So will we meet again? And will then hear how Günther Focke, not in Her Majesty's service, reveals facts that others try to hide! «, Miguel asked.

» Yes, us five will meet again! «, Arthur said and looked at Fiona, » if you feel like it, young lady, you are more than welcome to join us next time. The addresses and phone numbers were already given to you by a wise agent anyway. «

» It would be my pleasure, Arthur «, she said, » we are still young! And there are still lots of moments and places to discover! «

Marian opened the folding door and entered the drawing room with a candlestick.

» Gentlemen, Lady «, she said, » the rooms are at your disposal! «

To be continued …

From: Brigadier ████████████ C.B.E.

BUCKINGHAM PALACE

5th April, 1995

Dear Mr. Focke,

    Thank you for your letter of 2nd April in which you asked if it would be possible for you to come and see me to discuss a confidential matter.

    I am certainly prepared to consider seeing you and perhaps you would be kind enough to telephone me when we might arrange a suitable time. My telephone number is

Yours sincerely,

Mr. G. Focke

From: Brigadier ▓▓▓▓▓▓▓▓▓ C.B.E.

BUCKINGHAM PALACE

10th April, 1995

Dear Mr. Focke,

I am writing to confirm the arrangement we made on the telephone for us to meet at 11.30 a.m. on Wednesday, 19th April.

As you clearly wished our conversation to be confidential, I suggest that we should meet at my Club which is the Army and Navy Club, Pall Mall, London, SW1Y 5JG. The Club is on the corner of Pall Mall and St. James's Square. You will find that the entrance is just around the corner from Pall Mall in the Square.

This venue will certainly provide you with the confidentiality you seek but, at the same time, I would require you to bring with you some form of identification. A passport would be most suitable.

I look forward to seeing you on 19th April.

Yours sincerely,

Mr. G. Focke

From: Brigadier   C.B.E.

BUCKINGHAM PALACE

24th April, 1995

Dear Mr. Focke,

I appreciated meeting you on Wednesday, 19th April and having the opportunity to hear from you personally why you believe His Royal Highness The Duke of Edinburgh to be your father.

I am able to acknowledge receipt of the newspaper cuttings and the video you sent me as a result of our meeting. These are returned herewith.

Turning now to your proposition. You indicated that you were born in Wremen on 12th July 1946 and this is confirmed by the identity card you showed me. I have carried out investigations into Prince Philip's war service and I am able to confirm that, without any doubt whatever, His Royal Highness was on duty in H.M.S. Whelp in the Pacific without a break from the period of 2nd September when the Japanese surrender was signed in Tokyo Bay until H.M.S. Whelp's return to Portsmouth in early 1946.

The Duke of Edinburgh did not take any leave during this period and was certainly therefore not in Europe at the time when you would have been conceived.

These facts speak for themselves and I therefore suggest that you would be wise to seek elsewhere for your father's identity.

I believe this sets out the situation as it is quite clearly and would expect to hear no more of this matter either from you or in the Press.

Yours sincerely,

Mr. Günter Focke

BUCKINGHAM PALACE

17th April, 1997.

Dear Mr. Focke,

Thank you for your letter and enclosures of 10th March. The views you express in it concerning your parentage are noted, but I must reiterate the reply you were sent by The Duke of Edinburgh's Private Secretary, Brigadier on 24th April 1995 which refutes your allegation that His Royal Highness is your father. There is, therefore, nothing further which I can add to this information.

I am sending a copy of this reply to Brigadier so that he may know of your further approach to Buckingham Palace.

Yours sincerely,

Mr. Gunther Focke

MA (Oxon), MBA, Solicitor

Brigadier ███████ CVO, CBE
Duke of Edinburgh's Office
Buckingham Palace
London SW1A 1AA

Draft   Approved by Gunther
                    21/2/00

25 February, 2000

Dear Brigadier

His Royal Highness the Duke of Edinburgh and Mr Gunther Focke

I write as a friend of Mr Gunther Focke.

You will be aware that Mr Focke believes he is a son to His Royal Highness The Duke of Edinburgh. On April 24th 1995 you wrote to Mr Focke, as follows:

Dear Mr Focke

I appreciated meeting with you on Wednesday, 19th April (1995) and having the opportunity to hear from you personally why you believe His Royal Highness The Duke of Edinburgh to be your father. I am able to acknowledge receipt of the newspaper cuttings and the video you sent me as a result of our meeting. These are returned herewith.

Turning now to your proposition. You indicated that you were born in Wremen on 12th July 1946 and this is confirmed by the identity card you showed me. I have carried out investigations into Prince Philip's war service and I am able to confirm that, without any doubt whatever, His Royal Highness was on duty in H.M.S Whelp in the Pacific without a break from the period of 2nd September when the Japanese Surrender was signed in Tokyo until H.M.S. Whelp's return to Portsmouth in early 1946.

The Duke of Edinburgh did not take any leave during the period and was certainly therefore not in Europe at the time when you would have been conceived.

These facts speak for themselves and I therefore suggest that you would be wise to seek elsewhere for your father's identity.

I believe this sets out the situation as it is quite clearly and would expect to hear no more of this matter either from you or in the press.

Yours sincerely,

There is now clear evidence both that the Duke of Edinburgh returned to Europe shortly after the Japanese surrender, and also that he stayed at Balmoral early in September 1945, leaving it on 13th September 1945.

It may well be the case that Gunther Focke is not the Duke's son. However, Gunther has strong and convincing grounds for believing that he is, and his mind will not be set to rest until the issue has been determined conclusively. I am sure you will understand that any human being would be anguished by the situation Mr Focke finds himself in.

Paternity can be proved by simple blood tests. Indeed, His Royal Highness has already had his blood analysed and it would be a simple matter for him to agree to release details of his STR genotypes which have been recorded by Dr Peter Gill of the Central Research and Support Establishment, Aldermaston. It would be unreasonable for the Duke to refuse this request.

It is also possible to establish paternity by obtaining a blood sample from a true half-brother or half-sister.

There are legal procedures for requiring putative fathers to submit to paternity tests. I would refer to the Government's consultation paper entitled "Procedures for the Determination of Paternity", published in 1998 by the Lord Chancellor's Department.

I well understand that The Duke is frequently the subject of unfair accusation and that he cannot be expected to disprove every allegation that is made against him. Gunther's case, however, is different. The evidence is strong, and is now considerably further collaborated by your letter which is clearly intended to disguise the truth about the Duke's whereabouts at the time Gunther was conceived.

I hope you will not object unduly if I make the observation that actions associated with cover-up are frequently far more damaging than the matter they are designed to conceal. Furthermore, such actions tend to escalate in seriousness. I hope that will not be the outcome in Gunther's case.

I would be very grateful if you would show this letter to His Royal Highness and then contact me so that I may advise Gunther appropriately.

Yours sincerely

S D

Brigadier   CVO, CBE
Duke of Edinburgh's Office
Buckingham Palace
London SW1A 1AA

15 April, 2000

Dear Brigadier

His Royal Highness the Duke of Edinburgh and Mr Gunther Focke

I write further to my letter of 25th February and our telephone conversation of 8th March. Gunther is aware that you have been busy on a successful Royal tour. He is nonetheless keen to resolve matters speedily.

He is convinced that His Royal Highness the Duke of Edinburgh is his father. He has spent considerable time and effort collecting evidence to that effect. Given its weight it seems inappropriate merely to dismiss his assertions. If, however, they are incorrect they are easily disproved. Indeed, I did suggest in our telephone conversation that this might be achieved by finding a confidential third party who has the confidence of both parties who would be asked to compare blood chemistries. There is no good reason why the Duke should refuse this request given that his blood has already been analysed.

Now that Gunther also has clear evidence of intent to conceal the Duke's whereabouts at the time of his conception, he is wanting to force the issue by employing London solicitors, paid for by the media, to bring a paternity case. I have urged restraint and persuaded Gunther to let me intercede again.

I hope that it will be possible for the Duke to ask himself what else _he_ would do in Gunther's predicament. Gunther stresses that the proposed action would not be taken out of disloyalty. He can, however, think of no other way to bring matters to a head.

In the name of decency, compassion and fairness Gunther asks that the Duke either concedes privately that he might be his father or agrees to disprove the assertion so as to put Gunther's mind at rest. Not to do so merely continues a possible "cover up" which is potentially more damaging than the paternity issue itself.

Yours sincerely

- Copy.
- To be sent recorded delivery.
- Approved by Gunther 15/4/00

From: Brigadier   C.V.O., C.B.E.
Private Secretary to H.R.H. The Duke of Edinburgh

BUCKINGHAM PALACE

28th April 2000

Dear M.

I am replying to your letter dated 15th April and our conversation on the telephone on 18th April.

As I made clear in my letter to Mr. Focke dated 24th April, 1995, there is no doubt whatever that The Duke of Edinburgh, having joined H.M.S. Whelp in 1944, was on duty as First Lieutenant and Second-in-Command in the Ship in the Far East, without a break, from the signing of the Japanese surrender in Tokyo Bay on 2nd September, 1945, for which ceremony Whelp was anchored in Tokyo Bay. Subsequently, H.M.S. Whelp was deployed to Hong Kong and then Sydney eventually sailing to the United Kingdom in early 1946.

You allege as fact that "he stayed at Balmoral early in September 1945, leaving Balmoral on 13th September 1945". That is simply not true nor feasible given his presence in H.M.S. Whelp in the Far East at the time. It is significant you have not produced any evidence to back your allegation. You overlook or perhaps do not understand the fact that in 1945/6 the only way back from the Far East was by sea and that would have taken the best part of six weeks.

Whereas I have repeatedly explained that His Royal Highness was a serving officer at sea in the Far East at all relevant times of possible conception you are now making threats to take the matter to the media referring to evidence which you are not prepared to divulge or demonstrate.

Unless and until you have convinced me of that evidence I am not minded to ask His Royal Highness to authorise a release of any details relating to his STR genotype to which you made reference in your letter dated 25th February, 2000.

- 2 -

As a solicitor you will understand that a serious view is taken of the wholly unjustified allegation that Mr. Focke "has clear evidence of intent to conceal the Duke's whereabouts at the time of his conception". To date, you have not been prepared to produce or divulge any such evidence and therefore that allegation and the threats you make on behalf of Mr. Focke should be withdrawn. There must be no repetition or publication.

Yours sincerely,

Esq.

Brigadier   CVO, CBE
Duke of Edinburgh's Office
Buckingham Palace
London SW1A 1AA

1 May, 2000

Dear Brigadier

Thank you for your letter of 28th April, which I have shown to Gunther.

First, let me apologise for stating that His Royal Highness left Balmoral on 13th September 1945. Having now checked with Gunther, I find that the evidence shows he left there on 13th September 1946.

Gunther understands from *The Times* newspaper index that H.M.S. Whelp left Sydney on 2nd December 1945, arriving back in Portsmouth on 17th January 1946. You imply in your letter that the Duke was on the ship until its return. However, the following suggests that in fact the Duke left the ship early. (Gunther, incidentally, was conceived around 15th October 1945, give or take a two or three weeks).

1. Page 12 of a book by Louis Wulff, published by Sampson Low in July 1947, entitled "Elizabeth and Philip - our Heiress and her Consort" states:

    Back in 1945, when Philip came home from sea complete with beard it was, their friends averred, Princess Elizabeth who issued orders for him to shave it off".

2. Pages 60 and 61 of the German book by Heinz Cramer, published by Deutsche Buchvertriebs in 1956, entitled (in translation) "Elizabeth II and her sister Margaret Rose" (enclosed) state:

    On the evening after the signing of the [Japanese] surrender [2nd September 1945] uncle and nephew [ie Lord Mountbatten and the Duke] met up following the ceremony dinner on board [ship].

    "I find you have done sufficient duty abroad, Philip, and it would be good for you and your education if you would do duty back in England in the very near future. A good sea officer should have more than mere nautical skills. I will see if I can arrange for

you a command in your adopted home country".

Rarely has a nephew looked at his uncle with such pleasure, and rarely also has such an honoured person and a lieutenant captain of the British navy forgotten his discipline as did Philip at that moment. For he immediately ran to the radio station and called out to the radio operator, "Private telegram to London". And hours later, a telegram arrived at Buckingham Palace Post Office, being a telegram for her Royal Highness the Princess Elizabeth, which said, "Hope to be in England soon. Kind regards, Philip".

3. Gunther understands that a new first lieutenant joined H.M.S. Whelp about the time the Duke left it. The Duke remained on the manning list as a member of the ship, but the admiralty have confirmed to Gunther that that does not mean he necessarily remained on the ship in person.

4. Gunther has eye-witness German accounts of a high-ranking British officer visiting his mother both around the time of his conception and subsequently. According to those accounts, the officer was initially bearded but subsequently clean shaven. One of those witnesses clearly identified the person they saw as the Duke.

It is, incidentally, striking that you have not expressly denied that the Duke was in Germany in late 1945, nor have you said when he did arrive back in Europe.

It seems to me that the combined effect of the foregoing indicates:

1. The Duke did indeed return to Europe well before HMS Whelp. Officers of high rank typically made the journey home from the Pacific by way of boat to India and then 'plane. The duration of such journeys would not have been especially long.

2. The fact that the Duke is wanting to convey the impression that he did not arrive back in Europe before H.M.S. Whelp returned suggests there is a small chapter in his life he wishes to obscure.

3. The witness evidence in Germany and Gunther's physical similarity to the Duke at least raise a significant possibility that the Duke is Gunther's father.

Gunther believes that by allowing newspapers to publish his assertions witnesses will come forward who will either prove or disprove his beliefs (quite apart from possibly also funding litigation). However, he has asked me to repeat that he has no wish to go public with any of his views. He merely wishes to establish the truth, which can easily, painlessly and indeed anonymously, be established by comparison of STR genotypes.

It really does seem to me that it would be in everyone's interests (particularly in view of the assertions you make) if the question of paternity could be settled once and for all. The obvious inference will otherwise be that the Duke is afraid of the outcome.

I am away in France from 10th to 22nd May. A substantive reply prior to my leaving would assist me in persuading Gunther not to act unadvised in my absence.

I do, of course, repeat that it goes without saying that if the Duke does disprove paternity Gunther will owe him a considerable apology. However, so far the justification for providing that apology has been withheld.

Yours sincerely

Brigadier ███████ CVO, CBE
Duke of Edinburgh's Office
Buckingham Palace
London SW1A 1AA

3 May, 2000

Dear Brigadier ███████

I write further to my letter of 1st May.

Gunther now believes that the following chronology of events occurred:

1. In September 1945 the Duke returns to Europe, mainly by air. He is still bearded.
2. He goes to Northern Germany in October 1945 on official duties, during which time he meets Gunther's mother. This is probably in the *Schwanewedel* beer house in Wremen, which was in the English occupied zone and a favourite haunt of English servicemen. Gunther's mother was then 23 years old, dark haired, and apparently very attractive. She worked at the beer house.
3. Gunther is conceived about 15th October 1945.
4. The Duke returns to England and loses his beard.
5. The Duke flies to Australia in good time for H.M.S. Whelp's departure for Portsmouth. He remains clean shaven.
6. Subsequently the Duke re-visits Gunther's mother, and also arranges for food parcels to be sent.
7. When Gunther's mother discovers the official engagement of the Duke to Princess Elizabeth she tells people that that is an end to matters.

I can confirm that I myself have now spoken to a former member of H.M.S. Whelp's crew. It is clear that following Gunther's earlier assertions to the Press the Duke was keen to prove his presence in the Pacific. As a result, in 1995 Lieutenant Commander Lambert approached ex-crew members of H.M.S. Whelp to invite them to a re-union at which the press would be present. Initially, I understand, seven members were due to meet the Duke, but this number fell to three. This caused some concern. The Lieutenant Commander was therefore especially keen to ensure attendance, offering to pay all expenses, and even telephoning unsolicited late at night.

Gunther very much hopes that in view of the foregoing the Duke will now agree to a paternity test, even if only to disprove these allegations.

Yours sincerely

From: Brigadier   C.V.O., C.B.E.,
Private Secretary to H.R.H. The Duke of Edinburgh

BUCKINGHAM PALACE

19th May, 2000.

Dear Mr.

MR. GUNTHER FOCKE

Thank you for your letters of 1st and 3rd May.

What you have written in these letters does not remotely amount to evidence. You refer to some hearsay and inaccurate gossip journalism. There is no evidence at all to support the chronology of events alleged in your second letter.

You continue to ignore the plain facts. These are that The Duke of Edinburgh did not return from the Far East and the Pacific until H.M.S. Whelp arrived back in mid January 1946. His Royal Highness was nowhere near Europe at the relevant time.

The sentence you quote from Wulff's book is completely wrong. The year was 1946, not 1945 and Prince Philip was already clean shaven when he returned in January 1946. As to the Cramer extract, this, I understand, is a total fabrication. No such meeting or conversation took place. Wulff and Cramer do not amount to evidence for anything.

In your letter of 15th April you said you had evidence. In reply I asked you to show me that evidence. You have not surprisingly been unable to do so because His Royal Highness was not and could not have been in Europe at the time.

.../

This correspondence must now be terminated. You have at least now accepted your Balmoral date was a year out. However, despite having had the facts repeatedly made clear to you, it is noted you are still making threats. You and your client should not underestimate or ignore the last paragraph in my letter of 28th April.

Yours sincerely

Stephen Barnes, Esq.

MINISTRY OF DEFENCE
3-5 Great Scotland Yard, London SW1A 2HW

Telephone (Direct Dialling) 071-218   ) Ext 5451
         (Switchboard)   071-218 9000)

NAVAL STAFF DUTIES (HISTORICAL SECTION)

G. Focke	Your Ref: Fax 24 Nov 94
56 Dorking Walk	
Corby	Our Ref: D/NHB/9/2/17/IJA
N/HANTS	
NN18 9JN	Date : 24 November 1994

Dear Mr Focke

Thank you for your fax relating to the movements of HMS WHELP. Having checked our records here, I can confirm that the logs relating to the WHELP have not been preserved. I have however, been able to ascertain her movements after leaving Tokyo on 9 September. I attach a copy.

Lieutenant
Royal Navy

From: Naval Historical Branch
MINISTRY OF DEFENCE
Room 303, 3-5, Great Scotland Yard, London SW1A 2HW

Telephone (Direct dial) 020 7218 5451
(Switchboard) 020 7218 9000
ask for ext 85451
Fax 020 7218 8210

Mr G Foche,
24 Westminster Walk,
Corby,
Northants,
NN18 9JA.

Your Reference

Our Reference D/NHB/22/2

Date 22 . February 2001

Dear Mr Focke,

Thank you for your fax of 25 January 2001 and subsequent phone call regarding the WHELP.

I am sorry that you have not yet had a reply but, as I explained, for a variety of reasons I am having difficulty getting round to answering letters at the moment. Hopefully, I shall be able to answer your fax in the next few weeks.

Yours sincerely,

From: Naval Historical Branch
MINISTRY OF DEFENCE
Room 303, 3-5, Great Scotland Yard, London SW1A 2HW

Mr G Focke,
24 Westminster Walk,
CORBY,
Northants.
NN18 9JA

Our Reference: DNHB/22/2

Date: 8 March 2001

Dear Mr Focke,

As promised on the phone earlier this week, I am now replying to your fax of 23 January 2001 and your subsequent phone call regarding the WHELP.

The movements of the ship from June 1945 until she was laid up the following year, as recorded in the Movements Book, are shown below. Entries in the other columns are also shown. Entries in the Remarks column are shown separately.

DATE OF ARRIVAL	PLACE	DATE OF DEPARTURE	AUTHORITY FOR MOVEMENT ARR	DEP
Not shown	Manus	18 Mar 45		OD
Not shown	Tokyo	9 Sep 45		(Entry Indecipherable)
13 Sep 45	Hong Kong area	Not shown	ETA 140553Z/11	
Not shown	Sydney	6 Dec 45		0623442/12
Not shown	Fremantle	14 Dec 45		3007002/11 140850Z/12
28 Dec 45	Trincomalee	282135EF/12		
31 Dec 45	Aden	2 Jan 46	311822/12	020900C/1
5 Jan 46	Port Said	7 Jan 46	051651B/1	071650B/1
12 Jan 46	Gibraltar	14 Jan 46	141201A/1	172300Z/1
17 Jan 46	Portsmouth			

174

THE ROYAL NAVY

WHEATLAND.
Lieut.-Com., R.N.V.R. } R. G. Woodward (*act*)...... 14 Aug 45 (*In Command*)
Lieutenant............D. B. Holdsworth.......... 21 Aug 45
Tempy. Lieut., R.N.V.R. } J. F. N. Wedge............ 16 Aug 45
Lieutenant (E)....S. A. Nash (*act*)............ 10 Sept 45
Tempy. Sub-Lieut., R.N.V.P. } F. Kilburn................ 21 Aug 45
Tempy. Act. Sub-Lieut., R.N.V.R. } G. L. Rushton............... — Mar 45

WHELP.
Commander ......G. A. F. Norfolk.............. 28 Feb 44 (*In Command*)
● Lieutenant..........H.R.H. *Prince* Philip of Greece and Denmark.... 14 Feb 44
R. E. C. Hill.................. 14 Nov 44
P. Wareham.................. 3 Apr 44
Tempy. Lieut., R.N.V.R. } M. D. Hazell................ 29 Feb 44
Lieut.-Com. (E)...H. R. Kimber, MBE (*act*) ... 28 Apr 43
Tempy. Surg. Lieut., R.N.V.R. } O D. Fisher, MRCS, LRCP.. 12 Apr 44
Tempy. Sub-Lieut., R.N.V.R. } R. A. Hoskyn................ 1 May 45
B. E. Hardy................ 12 Apr 45
Tempy. Act. Sub-Lieut., R.N.V.R. } A. W. D. Gatrell............ — Sept 45
Gunner.............(T) G. W. Butler............ 16 Aug 45

WHIMBREL
Lieut.-Com........N. R. Murch .... 23 Nov 44 (*In Command*)
Lieutenant........P. M. Simpson................ 23 May 44
Lieutenant, R.N.R. } J. Bryant...................... — Apr 44
Lieutenant, R.A.N R. } A. F. Thornton (*act*)........ 1 Dec 43
Tempy. Lieut., R.N.V.R. } D. J. Mills.................. — Oct 43 (*In lieu of Specialist* (N) *Officer*)
Tempy. Sub-Lieut., R.N.V.R. { E. G. Shrosbree.............. 6 Oct 44
L. E. Nelson................ 8 Dec 44
H. G. Hughes................ 8 Dec 44
Tempy. Sub-Lieut. (E), R.C.N.V.R. { E. S. Smith .... 14 Sept 43
J. H. Richer................ 14 Sept 43
Tempy. Act. Sub-Lieut.(E), R.N.V.R. } G. F. Cooper................ 30 Aug 45
Cd. Mech.........H. R. White (*act*)............ 31 Oct 44

WHITAKER.

WHITE BEAR.
Captain..............A. Day, CBE................ (*In Command*)
Commander, R.N.R. } J. F. Drake................
Lieut.-Com.......K. W. Hay, DSC................
Lieutenant........N. D. Royds................
H. R. Hatfield................
D. W. Haslam................
Tempy. Lieut. (E), R.N.R. } F. E. Tonkin................
Lieut.-Com.(S)...D. H. Burgess................
Tempy. Surg. Lieut., R.N.V.R. } B. G. Hall, MRCS, LRC
Tempy. Sub-Lieut., R.N.V.R. } M. S. L. Joseph................
Boatswain..........G. A. Ryan................

WHITEHAVEN.
Tempy. Lieut.-Com., R.N.V.R. } W. J. Houghton, DSC (*act*)
Tempy Lieut., R.N.V.R. { G. A. Moritz................
J. S. Girvan................
Tempy. Surg. Lieut., R.N.V.R. } S. Moss, MRCS, LRCP......
Tempy. Sub-Lieut. R.N.V.R., } G. L Morrow................
Tempy. Wt. Engineer } J. W. Taylor................

WHITESAND BAY.
Lieut.-Com.........B. C. Longbottom (*act*) . (*In Command*)
Tempy. Lieut., R.N.V.R. } E. J. Bence................
Tempy. Sub-Lieut., R.N. } S. D. Gibson................
Tempy. Sub-Lieut., R.N.V.R. { P. Bullock................
C. W. Ford................
P. J. H. Vowles................
Tempy. Sub-Lieut.(E), R.N.V.R. } J. J. Wright................
Gunner.............C. P. Oliver (*act*)..........
Tempy. Mid., R.N.V.R. } R. F. Barclay................

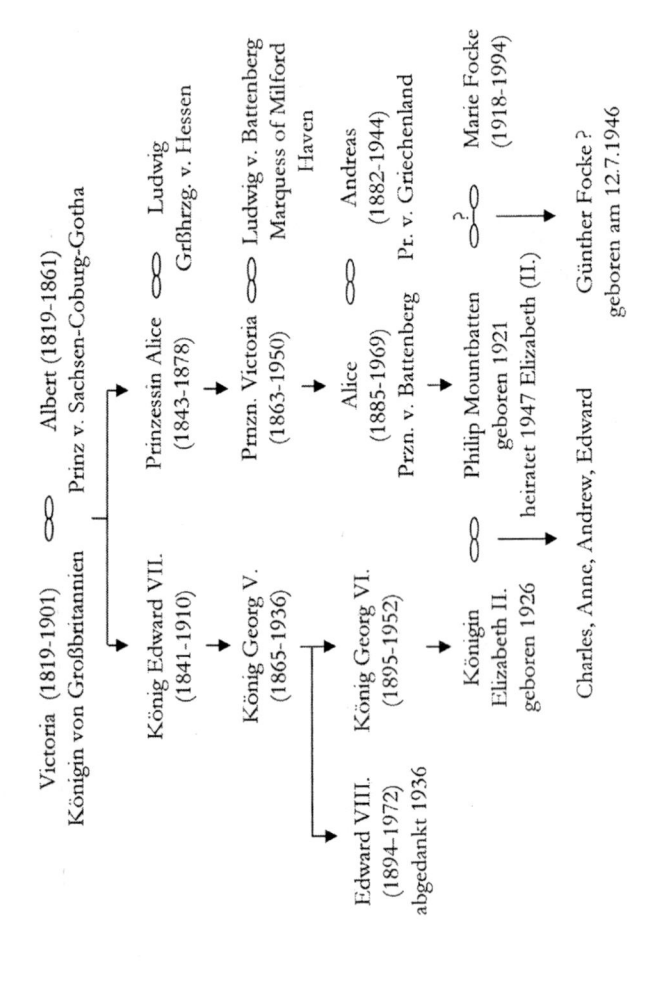

Victoria (1819-1901)　∞　Albert (1819-1861)
Königin von Großbritannien　　Prinz v. Sachsen-Coburg-Gotha

├── Prinzessin Alice (1843-1878) ∞ Ludwig Grßhrzg. v. Hessen
│   └── Prnzn. Victoria (1863-1950) ∞ Ludwig v. Battenberg Marques of Milford Haven
│   └── Alice (1885-1969) ∞ Andreas (1882-1944) Pr. v. Griechenland
│   └── Philip Mountbatten geboren 1921
│   heiratet 1947 Elizabeth (II.)

└── König Edward VII. (1841-1910)
      └── König Georg V. (1865-1936)
            ├── König Georg VI. (1895-1952)
            │   └── Königin Elizabeth II. geboren 1926
            │   ∞ Philip Mountbatten
            │   Charles, Anne, Andrew, Edward
            └── Edward VIII. (1894-1972) abgedankt 1936

Marie Focke (1918-1994) ∞ ?
→ Günther Focke ?
geboren am 12.7.1946

176

Literature

Boothroyd, Basil
Prince Philip – An Informal Biography, 1971
- Brandreth, Gyles
Philip und Elisabeth – Portrait einer Ehe, 2005
- Cramer, Heinz
Elisabeth II., 1957
- Dean, John
HRH Prince Philip – A Portrait, 1954
- Heald, Tim
The Duke – A Portrait, 1954
- Jugoslawien, Alexandra von
Prince Philip – A. Family Portrait, 1959
- Palmer, Alan
Gekrönte Vettern – Deutscher Adel auf Englands Thron, 1989
- Stuker, Jürg
Die Grosse Parade – Glanz und Untergang der Fürsten Europas, 1971
- Vickers, Hugo
Alice, Princess Andrew of Greece, 2000
- Wulff, Louis
Elizabeth and Philip – Our Heiress and Her Consort, 1947

Printed in the United Kingdom
by Lightning Source UK Ltd.
134608UK00001B/13-21/P